Spirit Quest

Katie Cruickshank

Katie Cruickshank

First published by Dog Ear Publishing
4010 W. 86th Street, Ste H
Indianapolis, IN 46268
www.dogearpublishing.net

ISBN: 978-1-4575-2166-9

This book is printed on acid-free paper.

Printed in the United States of America

For My Classmates:
You inspired me with your character and made
<u>Spirit Quest</u> come to life.

For Mrs. Bolin:
Without my Grammar Guru,
this would've never seen print.

For Aran:
Thanks for letting me express myself through you
and your journey.

TABLE OF CONTENTS

CHAPTER ONE

My Story

Run, *run!* The hunter was near. *Faster, faster!* I thought frantically as I accelerated. The hunter was fast. I looked over my shoulder. Shadow and Demon, my older brothers, were close behind me, breathing hard. I looked forward once more and concentrated. *Peoooooow!!!* A bullet grazed my shoulder. I stumbled and plowed into the snow.

I quickly rose and whipped around, heading into a more thickly wooded piece of land, where the hunter couldn't follow. My brothers ducked in behind me. We were safe, for now.

My name is Wilder. About a month ago, our parents died. It was hard at first, and still is, but we're healing. Of our character, I have little to say save for this: I may be a bit devious, but I'm still young. Demon is our main provider, a true hunter to the end. Shadow is the brains of the operation, but I help occasionally. Together, we make a good team, and we survive.

Our home, Arkamish, is surrounded by the Sea of Tears to the south, with the Deep Forest and the Spirit Mountains to the north. It is divided into the Wolf Realm and the Human Realm; humans hug the sea while we wolves cling to the safety of the mountains. To the east is Arcaña, where the wild horses prosper. To the west are Skye Haven and Dark Water, inhabited by others of our kind.

"I told you we were too close to the border! But no, you insisted that we follow that game trail south of it!" I accused Demon. In this family, we also argue. Frequently.

"You want us to starve? That was our best lead in a week!" Demon replied. "You think we can live on air and water, brainless?"

I growled and attacked him. We rolled around on the ground for several minutes before Shadow broke us up.

"Stuff it, Demon!" Shadow said. And as I shot Demon a triumphant glare, Shadow wheeled on me. "And you! You've scared away all the game for miles with your howling!" So, we left the grove to look for food.

Eventually, we found a couple of roe deer, successfully hunted, and ate. We settled down to rest. After a while, I smelled a change of weather coming. A blizzard, to be precise, likely the last one of the season. I roused my brothers and informed them. We decided we should move, because there were several large branches. It would be too easy for one to break and fall on one of us, even in a mild blizzard.

We found a cave, the entrance a few feet from a steep slope that dropped to a deep river crusted with ice. Our problem: a giant Kodiak. And it was angry. Without thinking, I charged. I leapt and clung to its leg, but it swatted me away like a fly. Shadow and Demon ran to my aid, but both slipped and slid into the coppice. The grizzly had me cornered, pushed against some brush in front of the slope.

The bear took a step. It took another step. I felt a branch pinned beneath me that would snap back into the bear's face if I somersaulted backward. That would mean, however, that I would fall down the slope to the river. The bear growled. Funny, those teeth convinced me it was worth the risk. I flipped down the slope as the branch did its job.

"Ooooooffff!" I grunted as I hit the icy riverbank. I backed up a yard or two, and my hind paw slipped through the ice. I gasped. I didn't think it was going to be that thin! The bear padded down the hill. The ice groaned, and a little crack started toward me. I looked down at the crack as the bear put its full weight on the ice. Too much. The bear went down, and the ice under my feet tilted. It started to flip. I scrambled toward the top, but I was slipping fast. Too fast. Then I was in the water.

Shadow and Demon slid down to the river just as I went in. They saw me through the ice and started to claw at the surface, but it was no use. The river's current was rapidly carrying me downstream. I was losing air, and I needed to surface. Then, I noticed the thin patch of ice I had slipped through. Desperately, I fought the current, but it wasn't enough. I passed out. Shadow and Demon saw what I had been trying to do and ran down the bank. When they were above me, Demon dove in the water. Seconds later, he brought me to the surface. I shivered like crazy as they dragged me to the cave.

CHAPTER TWO

Legend

We were lucky to have some talented friends with us. Lily, her older sister Rose, and Bibbles are our traveling companions. Lily and Rose are Arctic flower fairies, and Bibbles is their pet. Bibbles is a Burple, very similar to a tiny pink and yellow striped kitten with wings and antennae. Lily is the healer, and Rose has the brains. Working together, they fixed me up.

"Rose, what do we need to prevent hypothermia and pneumonia and to clean up that bullet graze?" asked Lily urgently.

"Fur weed, wild grasses, and birch fennel," Rose barked.

Bibbles zoomed away, returning within a few minutes. Lily did her work quickly. Finally, I was left alone. I looked around at the cave. It was big enough that we all fit into it, and there was still some extra space, so Demon made a few kills: three rabbits and four squirrels. He shoved them in a block of snow. Then, he and Shadow

5

made a brush pile in front of the entrance, as a barrier to the biting winds and icy snow to come. Then, all of us–the wolves and the parka-clad fairies–huddled up and slept.

Hours later, we awoke to the sounds of a howling demon as the blizzard raged on. Soon, we had a nice fire going and warmed some of the meat. The fairies made a stew of the squirrels and rabbits, seasoned with thyme, rosemary, and sage. It was good and quickly replenished my strength. We sat around and talked about herbs, sicknesses, and old legends and hunting stories. This was the best part. I requested the Legend of Aran, my favorite. In a deep voice, Shadow began.

"Once, on a cold, cold winter's night, there was a wolf named Rhans who gave birth to her first pup, Aran. Aran was a silver wolf, one of the first in the world. He proved to be intelligent and soon began to grow wings and develop fire-breathing skills and other spiritual features. Now, Rhans gave birth to many other pups and each of them in addition to having spiritual features was a silver wolf. They soon bonded other creatures, creating the many different spirits. The husband of Rhans, Haven, had another mate, Shilure, and they were proud of all of the pups, but they favored three: Aran the Silver Wolf Spirit, Hacea the White Wolf Spirit, and Shetvan the Grey Wolf Spirit. These three were the wisest of all the pups and the most powerful.

"Shetvan, however, was a brutal warrior with a savage temper, and died in a great battle before all the others. Aran and Hacea were great leaders and fair ones as well. The two were skilled fighters and wiser than any being. They died last of old age and wounds. There was a great sadness that swept the land, and our people wept. Shetvan and Hacea, as well as their many siblings have returned, but Aran remains lost. A wise prophet by the name of Shelim told them not to weep. He and his brother, Daran the Hunter, both sons of Shilure, kept the people of Arkamish's hopes alive with news of Aran's return. Someday, he will return," Shadow finished, his voice full of hope.

"Yes. Someday he will return!" I agreed.

"Yeah, he will someday, little bro," Demon smiled, ruffling my fur.

"You wanna roughhouse, you get roughhoused right back, DUMBON!" I growled, jumping at Demon. Shadow soon joined in the scuffle.

We wrestled for a couple minutes before Lily yelled, "Hey, guys, cut it...AAAAHHHH! WATCH IT!" She narrowly avoided getting squashed by someone's paw. And if looks could kill, this wolf would be dead! Demon poked his head out, grinning.

"Sorry, girls. This nutcase," he gestured at me, "started it. I had to do something."

I growled, "Why, you…" I started forward. Shadow stopped me.

"Wilder, come on! He's just fooling around," he said, giving Demon an angry glare.

Demon smirked apologetically. We told a few more stories and ate again as the blizzard blew itself out. As the weather settled, we decided to move on. The fairies banked the fire, and Shadow, Demon, and I tore down the wall of branches. Then, we set out once more.

As we continued, I stopped to sharpen my claws on a tree and to scent the air. I smelled human. At the same time, Demon and I thought out loud, "Hunter, or some-one looking for fighting wolves." I grinned as we exchanged a surprised look. We decided to split up; Bib-bles and I went north, Lily and Demon went south, and Shadow and Rose went east. I walked for a few miles, and finding nothing, decided to find Shadow.

When we met up, we found another bear, but this one went after Shadow. I'd love to say I single-handedly brought it down and saved the day, but honestly, I turned tail and hid behind a tree. It picked up Shadow and threw him against another tree. Instead of going for the kill, the bear walked over to investigate something in the brush. Quickly, I pulled Shadow behind my tree. The bear lum-bered away. Shadow groaned. I sent Bibbles after Demon and Lily.

"Wilder, get some fur weed. It will act as a painkiller," ordered Rose.

Quickly, I retrieved the herb. We watched and waited. Shadow's life was now in Bibbles's hands.

Meanwhile, Demon was having some problems of his own. The man we had smelled had cornered him. Demon gave in after a fight, allowing himself to be muzzled and tied to the sled. The man drove his team to Stamaruak, the nearest human town, and went inside the tavern. Lily, who had been hiding in the sled, quickly untied Demon's attachments just as Bibbles arrived. Urgently, the trio raced back to find Shadow and me.

CHAPTER THREE
Ghosts of the Past

B efore they arrived, something weird happened. The wind picked up until it was screaming, and then it faded away. As it reached a cool, gentle breeze, it brought a familiar scent. Not Demon, Lily, or Bibbles, though. "Oh…my…lords," I swore.

"Um…Wilder, are those your…parents?" asked Rose.

I nodded.

"Okay," she murmured and then promptly fainted. She and her sister had been close friends with our parents and were devastated by their deaths.

"Wilder? Are you alright? Is that…oh, lords!" The voice of my mother cursed.

"Mom? Is that you!?!" I exclaimed, unbelieving, as I whipped around. There were my parents, in ghostly outlines. "Why are you here now?" I asked, tears in my eyes.

"To warn you, Wildy. And to check on him," Dad said, nodding at Shadow.

"He's been wandering...where we are now," Mom explained uneasily.

"You mean... ," I started. They nodded.

"But the others are almost here. He'll be fine, Wildy," reassured my mother. "And in the meantime, sing 'The Song of the Spirits', and the spirits will guide you. We have to go now, Wildy; we're out of time," said my mother, kissing me on the forehead.

"And Wilder, don't forget; we'll always be there if you need to talk to us," offered my father.

They shimmered and disappeared.

Suddenly, Demon and the others burst out of the brush. "Wilder! Where's Shad...Ah, I see," Demon murmured, biting his lip.

"Quit standing around! We have work to do!" ordered Lily. She sprang into action. "Bibbles, fetch some birch bark, silver stem berries, and fire opal petals! Now!" ordered Lily, after exchanging a knowing glance with her sister, who had regained consciousness.

Bibbles zoomed off.

When Bibbles returned, the fairies quickly mashed the herbs into a paste, mixed the paste with boiling water, and spooned it into Shadow's mouth. He groaned and stirred; nothing more. We sat waiting for a few tense minutes as I told Demon what had occurred. Abruptly, Shadow raised his head, coughing and sputtering. I sighed in relief.

"Easy, Shadow, easy. Not so quickly!" scolded Lily.

"I…will not…take it…easy!" Shadow growled. He rose and staggered.

"Slowly, Shadow. Slowly. Everything's going to be all right," I instructed.

"Well, I hope you can walk, you big oaf, 'cause I'm not carrying your sorry hide!" Demon said, smirking disdainfully.

"Why, you little swine!" Shadow cussed.

He then flabbergasted us all, especially Demon, by leaping at the offender and cuffing him. Seeing that Shadow was obviously quite well, we began planning. We knew we had to go to the Spirit Mountains to find a new place to call home. But that wasn't the only reason.

There was an uprising that was dangerously close to erupting into civil war between the rebel army, led by the unicorn Kalabar, and the much-scorned Shetvan. It had been sparked by Shetvan's refusal to assist his subjects in the famine of the last season. Our parents had been great supporters of Kalabar's cause until their untimely deaths. My brothers and I felt that we should petition the kinder Hacea to negotiate with Kalabar and prevent the war. Unfortunately, we'd have to cross the Devil's Horne, a treacherous ridge of rock and ice, and half the Deep Forest, to reach her castle, Wildspirit.

After we had hunted a young buck and eaten, we began the long trek. At midnight, we arrived at the Devil's Horne. As did the feeling we were being watched. Suddenly, I pounced. In my paws, I caught a rabbit.

"This will make a delicious dessert!" I told the others after I'd delivered a mercy stroke.

My brothers licked their lips as we dug in. Then, we proceeded upward, carefully watching our steps. However, as we ascended, so did the prickly feeling on the back of my neck.

We were about three-quarters of the way up the trail when my foot twisted in sudden pain. "Arrrrrrrhhhhh-hggg!" I had been bitten by a mountain snake! "Lily! Hurry!" I yelled.

"Bibbles! Fourteen palhiochas petals! Quickly!" Rose demanded.

Bibbles zipped off. Meanwhile, the snake was struggling with Demon.

"Sssssstop! My name is Surdel! I thought you were sssssspies!" he hissed desperately.

"Spies?" I choked before blacking out. I would have to wait until morning to learn what he had meant.

CHAPTER FOUR

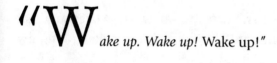

Of Spies & Secrets

"**W**ake up. *Wake up!* Wake up!"

"What!" I shouted petulantly.

"Good. You're up, you couch potato!" Demon said.

"You woke me up for that? I rumbled indignantly. "Moron!" I rose without delay to punish my brother. My left fore ankle twisted and sparked. "OOOOOOWWWWWW!" I yelped.

Shadow grinned. "Hey, knucklehead," he scolded, knocking me on the head. "Remind that little rock in there you're hurt!"

I growled, cussed, and limped away, muttering.

Very quickly, the fairies patched me up with an endless procession of herbs, poultices, and wraps. I shortly began to walk on the limb again, if somewhat restrictedly. We proceeded to interrogate the prisoner, whom Lily had bound.

I limped to the snake. "Why did you think we were spies? Who did you think we were working for? And who are *you* working for?" I demanded.

"Um…er…because a rebel isss launching attacksss on His Majesty'sss castle. The rebel. And…of course…er…His Majesty," Surdel responded, befuddled.

"Surdel, we aren't daft. We know 'His Majesty' is that lewd traitor Shetvan!" I informed the snake, rolling my eyes at his lack of intellect.

"Please! Don't use hisss name that way!" pleaded Surdel, looking around like a frightened rabbit. "He could be anywhere!"

That's when I realized something important. "Guys, could you come over here a sec?" When everyone was gathered around, I said, "Okay. We all know Shetvan is the king, right?" Everyone nodded. "We all know 'The Song of the Spirits', right?" Again, everyone nodded. "So Shetvan, Hacea, and Aran are featured in the *third* verse, and my brothers & I are *three* wolves!" I exclaimed, bursting with excitement.

"Wilder! You're a genius! I should have known. The song is a map!" Shadow said.

"I bet that's what Mom and Dad meant when they said to remember 'The Song of the Spirits' and they'll guide you!" piped up Demon. Suddenly, he looked up. "Oi! Where'd that little worm go!" he exclaimed.

Surdel had bitten through his bonds and was escaping! Within seconds, Demon had the struggling snake under his paws.

"You're Shetvan's spy, aren't you?" I spat.

"Yesss! Yesss! Please...don't kill me!" Surdel gasped.

"Does Shetvan know we're coming, snake?" I snarled. Surdel quickly nodded yes. "Get out of my sight!" I growled.

Surdel slithered away, whimpering, "If Shetvan ever findsss out about thisss, he'll skin me alive!"

Gathering everyone around me, I announced, "If The Song truly is a map, then we should sing the rest of it."

We sang, "Let it rain upon you, like wind upon the sand. The ice plains are thinning, as the ice expands."

"What does that mean?" said Demon.

I glared at him. "The ice is thinning! Remember?" I spat, meaning the incident with the bear.

"How could I forget? Sheesh!" grouched Demon. "Next up: second verse. Daylight hours risk being seen. Travel during twilight's silver sheen."

"We should travel at night," Shadow said guiltily.

"The Spirits, our creators, wish to learn. Come to them before the ice burns. Before the ice burns? That doesn't make any sense...unless it means the war! We need to reach Wildspirit before the ice burns from the strain of the conflict!" I pointed out. "But what about the fourth verse?"

"One of three travelers, he's the missing name. He's the missing spirit, the last one of fame. Do you think one of us is Aran's descendant?" asked Shadow as he finished the verse.

"Could be," I shrugged.

"And what about the next verse?" asked Rose.

"He's favored by the sun and moon; he's favored by night & day. He's favored, oh, so greatly, at least that's what they say," sang Lily softly. "Well?" she asked her sister, "What about it?"

"I suppose it's correct. In most of the older stories, Aran created the sun and moon, and in return they gave him night and day," said Rose.

"So, let's recap: the ice is thinning, we should travel at night, the Spirits want us to reach them before the war, and one of us might be Aran's descendant," I proclaimed.

"Let's get some sleep," said Shadow.

"Let's eat first. I'm starving," I said. Everyone agreed heartily.

Slowly, but surely, I was changing. And everyone knew it. I was getting stronger, and unlike Shadow and Demon's red and black coats, I was developing a thick, gleaming silver coat. I was getting taller, getting stronger, and becoming a wiser wolf as I learned from the forest. Behind my back, everyone said, "I bet it's him!"

One day, I went hunting. As I was heading back to where the others were waiting, I knew something was wrong. I smelled smoke. I heard crackling and roaring. I felt the earth's vibrations beneath me. But I had no clue what it was. I had never smelled this kind of smoke or heard this kind of crackling or roaring. The only things I felt from the earth were "Faster! Danger! Fear!" I raced back to the clearing where the others were, just as it burst into flames. A huge dragon was attacking my brothers. Filled with a mad sort of rage, I leapt at the creature's back and bit the base of its neck hard. It roared angrily as I shot away. I wasn't a moment too soon. As I rolled off, the barbed, poisonous tail hit the spot where I had been seconds before. The beast turned toward me. I leapt at its chest, but was thrown to the ground.

"Run! I'll catch up!" I shouted, clambering toward the dragon's jugular.

"We won't leave you!" Shadow roared fiercely.

"Shadow, go," I pleaded softly, my eyes locking with his.
Shadow opened his mouth as if to argue, then bit his lip. Looking down and away, he signaled to Demon, and they fled. I finally ripped open the dragon's throat and bit so hard it hurt. But before I could react, the barbed tail slashed open my leg. The poison swept through my bloodstream.

I ran. Ran so fast I could've broken the sound barrier. I stopped once I reached a hollow surrounded by many trees, breathing so hard it hurt. In the hollow, I discovered a small rock overhang just big enough for me to slide under. My head spun as I spit up some sick, then lapped up water from a trickle of water that carved into the overhang's side. The cool liquid poured down my stinging throat. I was overcome with feverish dreams.

I woke up, panting as I gazed at the starry sky for the beast. Save for the moon, nothing gazed back at me. No creature of fear and pain. Lords…the dread beast of lore I'd heard about as a cub was real. A real, twisted nightmare! I thought about the dragon, and there was a lot to remember. He had been a golden color with black eyes and scarlet irises. He had long, sharp ivory claws and a reddish-gold flame. His wings were golden and leathery. I thought I heard a faint wing beat, but dismissed it as a dream. Out of anger, shock, and sadness, I howled at the ageless moon.

I let my feelings get the better of me; I should not have howled. As I returned to the ledge, I heard a distinct wing beat. The dragon had returned. It had come for me.

As I leapt to turn around, the poison sped through me, as did dizziness. The dragon descended slowly. I was weakening as the toxin fulfilled its purpose. Swiftly, the drug coursed through my bloodstream, causing more damage with each heartbeat. I used the majority of my strength to bite the dragon one last time, before leaping over it and stumbling toward the edge of the clearing. I heard the ledge exploding as I dropped at the very fringe of the coppice, exhausted. The last thing I remember were his claws cradling me. Then, we took off into the velvety night sky, and I blacked out.

CHAPTER FIVE

Dragon Secrets

I woke up to a flash of gold light, the discovery that my leg was cured, the midday sun shining on me, and a ravenous hunger! I jumped up and shook myself into alertness. The remains of a deer carcass lay in front of me. A deep voice startled me as the dragon bade me welcome.

"You are awake. That is good."

"Where are my brothers? What am I doing here? Who are you? And where am I?" I snarled, crouching and ready to fight.

The dragon was amused. "Peace," he chided. "Your companions are safe. You are here to be taught. I am Apache, son of Wind Chaser. You are," he said, gesturing with a keen talon, "in Dracor's Nest, my home."

I continued to eye him warily.

"Now, please eat! I will not have you starve under my wing."

I stepped forward and began to eat ravenously, all the while watching him with one eye.

"The forest has taught you well, Wilder," the dragon said quietly.

I froze. "How did you know my name? And as far as teaching goes, the forest is open to those who will listen, as I have," I said, respecting him a bit more.

"I know these things. I have been about and learned from it," Apache replied.

My curiosity got the better of me. I sighed. "Well, where do we start, then?"

"The beginning, naturally," said Apache. "You are spirit of wisdom, hope, courage, and strength, the Spirit of the Silver Wolf, also known as Aran or the Night Warrior. You have the ability to read the earth and see without your eyes." Here he paused to allow questions. His revelation stunned me into speechlessness. He continued. "You created the sun and moon, and they gave you night and day in return. You created all things, beings, animals, and life with the help of the Mutari, the horse spirits of evil and goodness. You died and were reborn a wolf-pup as the phoenix dies and rises in the living ash. You were revived and lived the life that is told in the legend. As you died in that form, you rose again in your current form, as the cycle repeats itself, and I know not what has transpired since then." He exhaled and waited for me to respond.

I was in total shock. *I was the lost spirit?* "What...but that's...what do you mean?" I sputtered, struggling to absorb the information heaved upon me. "Do you mean to say," I said, struggling to control my thoughts, "that I...am Lord Aran? I mean, we knew there was a chance...but that's preposterous! THAT'S IMPOSSIBLE! I AM WILDER FREERUNNER!" I roared, my thoughts bursting out of my skull, forming a swirling storm of fury. I took a breath, calming myself, forcing myself to hide it away. I relaxed. Of course, I didn't believe him entirely. "I'm sorry, Apache. My tongue speaks of its own free will."

"Quite all right, Wilder. I was once young and rash as you are now. Still am, as a matter of fact," he smiled roguishly. "But could you please commence in telling your story, from where I left off?"

"It would be my pleasure," I smiled. I began with telling him of the rich, warm smell of the den as I had opened my eyes for the first time; the pride my parents and I felt when I caught my first rabbit; lessons in hunting with my mother and Demon; lore and history with my father and Shadow; the lessons of the forest with my mother, my father, and myself. Eventually, we came to the event of my parents' deaths. Here I slowed; I wished to tell this story only once.

"My mother, Klemore, was a beautiful, dark-reddish color, with gold, laughing eyes. She was always watchful of me, as I turned out to be the most reckless and mischievous. About a month and a half ago, I stole off during a game of Find the Lost Lord. However, my hiding place was so good, they couldn't find me until my mother, the master tracker, joined the search. She was scared I was hurt, or worse, so I wasn't too surprised that she grounded me for a week.

"The day after I had fulfilled my sentence was my birthday. From Shadow and Demon, I got a book called *Sword Lore*. From Mom and Dad, I got a new Stone Alpha set. Allow me to explain. You have either twelve black or twelve white wolves made of stone. There are 32 black paw prints and 32 white paw prints in a checkerboard pattern (called lopes), and the wolves are set up in two rows. One pack has to capture the other pack's wolves. Each wolf can move only one lope in any direction, except for the alpha male and female, which can move three lopes in any direction. The alphas are designated by the high carriage of their tails. The male has sapphire eyes, the female topaz.

"I also got permission to go see Star, my <u>very</u> close girl-friend across the river, if I was careful. However, I lost track of time because we were busy doing…grown-up stuff. Anyway, a blizzard was brewing. My father Shamar, a huge black wolf with piercing silver eyes, sent my brothers to look for me and bring me home. They found me, but halfway home, the blizzard struck, so we had to shelter in a small cave.

"My parents, worried, journeyed as far as the river. There, they were forced to make a snow shelter. They attempted to keep each other warm, but the blizzard was too strong, and…they…," I choked, and the hot tears streamed down my face. I could not go on.

"I have caused you pain, and for that I am sorry. I shouldn't have pushed you so soon," Apache apologized softly, then left me to my sorrow.

After a few minutes, I forced myself to take some deep breaths.

"My father would not want my emotions to interfere with my work. I am ready," I told Apache, wanting to hear more.

"You are wise beyond your years, Aran. I shall begin my tale now. One day during a hunt, I came across the two lesser spirits plotting against you. Hacea," he spoke the name vehemently, "was with Shetvan, griping about the unfairness of you having power and not knowing how to use it properly. I've been looking for you since, in case they tried to find you.

"You," he said gravely, "must know things to understand what you must do in this cycle before you can accomplish it. You must defeat your adversaries, in this case, the White Wolf Spirit, spirit of trickery, strength, hope, and boldness, who was on your side." Here, he paused to say, "Traitor!" under his breath. "And The Grey Wolf Spirit, spirit of boldness, courage, slyness, and retribution. You will soon begin to transform in the nights, but they will be only half-transformations."

"Will I be dangerous?" I inquired, worried.

"Only to those you choose to be dangerous to, as you are taking on your true spirit form," Apache replied. My stomach growled. I looked up and saw it was nearly dusk. I hadn't realized it would take quite this long to talk.

"Apache, perhaps it would be wise to hunt now. It has been a long day…," I said, hinting that I was speaking from my stomach.

"I believe it would be," Apache replied with a playfully wry smile.

I returned his grin before pausing to feel the earth. *A small herd of reindeer, woods, just north!* I took off, running smoothly and conservatively. I circled them, waiting to catch Apache's eye. I finally succeeded in doing so and mouthed the words, *On three.* He nodded, and I began to count in my head. *One, two…three!*

I leapt out and tailed a doe and her large fawn as Apache dove and seared a young buck to a crispy consistency. I ran ahead of my pair, made a hairpin turn around a log, and the fawn ran right into my waiting jaws. With ease, I dragged her over to Apache. The deer was a perfectly sized meal, and I snapped it up in five minutes.

Apache and I shared some spectacular hunting stories before, with a full stomach, he said, "We should return to Dracor's Nest, my friend. The shadows lengthen."

"I agree with you," I assured him with a hearty laugh. We began to lope to his stony cliffside home. Deep in thought, I closed my eyes, trusting my paws to guide me. The seconds turned to minutes as the silence stretched onward. Finally, I spoke. "Apache, I must leave to find my brothers tonight."

Apache was worried and surprised. "Are you mad? You can't go out there at night! There are too many dangers!"

"*That* is exactly why I have to go!" I argued. Apache sighed.

"As you wish," Apache replied, beaten.

"Don't be so worried about me, Apache! I can fend for myself. Trust me," I said.

"That doesn't mean it's not dangerous out there!" he snapped. "If you die tonight, I could never forgive myself!"

"I promise, I'll be careful, Apache. I do!" I insisted.

"All right. Tell your brothers I'm sorry I attacked them. I just had... ,"

"Jumpy nerves?" I supplied with a smirk. He stared at me. Interesting. It appeared I could see into his mind. "Farewell, Apache. Good hunting," I said, disappearing into the Deep Forest.

I had so much energy for one who had run two miles. It felt like I was a young pup again! I had an urge to howl, and did. I immediately wished I hadn't. The unearthly, eerie howl, so unlike my own that I doubted it could have been mine, reverberated over the moonlit forest. Now, all sorts of dark creatures knew I was there; I was easy prey. However, I picked up a nearby howl that I identified as Shadow's, washing away all these morbid thoughts. My heart was full of joy as I responded and sped up.

Minutes later, we met, elated to see each other. My brothers had been worried sick when they had arrived at the clearing in time to see 'the beast' carry me off. I identified him as Apache and filled them in on what had occurred; however, as I still had my doubts, I refrained from mentioning his prophecy concerning my identity.

"Where are the other three?" I asked curiously, with a smile etched on my face. Shadow and Demon exchanged grim looks.

"We don't exactly know," Demon admitted reluctantly.

"What?" I demanded, the smile fading away.

"They were gone this morning when we woke; they haven't returned since," Shadow explained as gently as possible, putting a paw on my shoulder. With opportune timing, Apache arrived.

"Wilder, I came as soon as I could. I heard your howl," he said. "I saw the fairies on the way down. They are trapped in a cage hanging from a tree. Something else is there. Hurry!"

"Follow me!" I roared, already in motion. The other two responded with quick action.

"We're on your tail!" reported Demon.

I nodded, jumping a stream. As I rounded the turn going around a large tree, I pulled up, skidding in the dirt. My brothers slammed into me.

"Stay here in case I need backup," I instructed them. "But if I get into trouble, back off and follow it unless it tries to kill me immediately." As they began to protest, I said, "It won't do me any good if you get killed too, will it?"

Then, I entered the clearing. To my surprise, when the girls saw me, they gasped, and Lily began to sob, holding Bibbles.

"Wilder! You shouldn't have come! It's a trap! Run! Go! Get out of here, before it's too late!" Rose cried, clenching the bars with her tiny fists.

I was scared. Had Apache been telling the truth? Was this an attempt to kill me using the fairies as bait? Then Rose, the tough, cool-headed one, burst into tears. That scared me worse; I began to back up. Then, I tensed with the feeling I was being watched. Finally, I heard faint paw steps and saw shadows out of the corner of my eyes. I had to time only to yell, "Shadow! Demon! Run!" before, with a heavy *thunk*, I fell, muzzle first, into the snow beneath the blow of a club. A command was barked sharply, and I was retrieved by a soldier as I lost consciousness.

CHAPTER SIX

Prisoner

What? Where am I? I thought blearily as I rolled over and stood up, shaking myself. I looked around. I was being held in what would be a grey stone cell except that it only had three sides; one behind me and one on either side. I was lying on an old, faded rug. There was nothing between me and the corridor. Beyond it there was and a door marked **PRISONERS' FEED**, reminding me of my hunger. I gathered myself to spring, but inches away from my goal, I was stopped with a jolt.

Gingerly, I turned halfway around and saw the chains that held my hind legs to the walls. I had been captured by either Shetvan or Hacea! Suddenly, a soft tread of leather boots filled the hallway.

"Well, Captain Drake? Is he awake?" asked the most beautiful voice I had ever heard. It was mesmerizing, like looking in a poised snake's eyes.

"Yes, Ma'am. I heard him moving around back there," replied a gruffer voice. To my amazement, they were both dressed like humans and…hey, I guess Apache was right! I could see without my eyes!

His mistress walked toward my cell. She stopped in front of me, looking away. I growled, deep in my throat.

"How are we today, Wilder? Fine, I should think," she smiled lightly.

"Who are you?!" I snapped, already knowing the answer.

"You can call me Hacea." She looked up. She had a beautiful, deep-rust colored coat. Her eyes were a striking, seductive shade of sparkling copper. To my surprise, Hacea looked like my mother! She was wearing a deep green tunic, chinos, and cape with a silver lining. On her chest was her seal: a gold paw print and silver lightning bolt. Despite myself, I let out a soft wolf-whistle. What? I couldn't help myself! She was attractive! She smiled, almost shyly. "I was leaving, but I remembered you had to eat."

How nice of you! I thought, spellbound by her looks and the prospect of food. She looked at a panel of buttons and selected one. A haunch of deer meat and a bowl of fresh water slid into my cell.

"I will enjoy talking to you again in the morning, after my conference," Hacea told me as I stepped toward the food.

I will, too, I thought.

Then, with a flourish of her cape and a flick of her tail that tickled my nose, she turned and walked away.

Wow, she's hot, I thought, still a bit groggy. There must have been something in the water, because I was suddenly overcome with drowsiness, asleep before I hit the ground.

Arise. It is time. An ancient voice echoed in my head as I bounced to my paws.

"What? Who's there?" I asked sleepily, turning my head from side to side. *Hmmm, just my imagination*, I thought, yawning. For one who had just gotten up, my vision, scent, hearing, and mind were extraordinarily clear. And my throat was dry. And there was a refilled water bowl in front of me. As I stepped forward to drink, I closed my eyes and relaxed. When I opened them, despite the water's rippled surface, I could clearly see the transformation had come, silent and swift.

I don't even recognize myself! I thought, mortified. An opaque silver mask obscured my eyes and forehead, but I could still see unusually well. My seal, apparently a black paw print and cyan tongue of flame, was embroidered on a black leather vest, covering my chest. The remainder of my fur had a strange charcoal sheen, as if it was covered with shadow. My claws were as lightning, cutting through metal and bone. And to top it off, I had a pair of dragon's wings on my shoulders and a dragon's mouth, which quickly revealed the ability to breathe ice fire.

I gotta get out of here, I thought with a grin as I tested my wings. I sliced the shackles with my claws. I ran in circles around my cell; then, gaining enough speed, I tucked in my wings, bounded through the window, and unfurled my wings as I soared over the castle wall and toward the almost half-moon.

When I was just below the clouds on that cool evening, floating on a crisp breeze, I leveled out. I swung my head around, twirled, and looped as I became accustomed to freedom and flying all at once. I whooped excitedly as I twisted through the air like a slippery serpent. As I scanned the countryside surrounding the castle in which I had been held prisoner, I saw a flash of gold and zeroed in on it.

Apache? I thought. *Apache!* I quickly spiraled down toward him, thrilled to see him.

At last he saw me. "Wilder! What happened to you?" Apache asked, grinning.

"I got captured by Hacea, but then I transformed, like you said, so I got out and...what's wrong?" I asked as Apache frowned.

"You were captured by Hacea? That means she has some sort of tracking spell on you, which means...." He broke off thoughtfully.

I looked over my shoulder. "Which means I need to get back, because my wings are shrinking?" I suggested quickly.

With a look of horror on his face, he nodded. I hovered over him as he moved, and we began a speedy retreat to the castle.

On our way, Apache explained to me that as long as I was her prisoner, Hacea could track me or cause me to degenerate from this form. When we got to the wall, Apache panted, "This is as far as I can go! Hurry!"

I nodded my thanks to him and just managed to burst through the window before my wings disappeared. I hit the concrete floor hard. The wind was knocked out of me. I felt my senses dull to their normal state, my claws harden, and the vest disappear before my mouth lost its cold feeling and sharpened bite. I rearranged myself with a jerk, then I lost consciousness. My dreams were disturbed with copper eyes, blank faces, and voices haunting me in the dark.

In the morning, I discovered I had been moved from the cell into one of the many "guest" rooms inside the fortress. This one was specially designed for me, it seemed, as it was very dark. I was on a soft, square, dark green bed, surrounded by a canopy and curtains. My coat had been washed and groomed. I was wearing a black shirt and silver chinos. My seal was embroidered on the shirt in silver. How this had all happened without me waking up, I didn't know; I was generally a very light sleeper. This thought was soon chased from my mind as I smelled the carcass of a large rabbit. If I was not deceived, it was rolled in deer fat and splintered bone! I eagerly jumped off my bed, nudging the curtains aside. I alighted on a floor thickly carpeted with black bear furs. There was a small writing desk in one corner of the room, which was currently holding my breakfast!

After I consumed the meal and drained a flask of elderberry juice, I took another look around the room. The outside of the curtain (and indubitably the inside as well) was woven of steel threads, in a pattern of dark trees leering out of the murk, giving it a look of the forest at night. The room smelled like crushed pine needles. In the front left corner of the room, there was a small heated pool, about the size of a small pond, with rocks surrounding it. The walls were painted the same pattern as the curtains, but with an additional waist-high greenish mist. Also, three paintings of white dragons, very small, were clustered close to the door. I was about to jump in the water when the door opened, and Hacea walked in. I swore and replaced my pants, flinging my shirt under the bed.

"I'm sorry, I didn't mean to interrupt…," she apologized, looking the other way and blushing. She was wearing a cold blue shirt and soft, pastel green leggings with a silver circlet.

"No, it's my fault, really. I forgot you were coming," I said, shaking my shaggy head. I sat down on the bed, but she remained standing.

"If you don't mind, I would like to show you a few things around the room," Hacea began.

I nodded eagerly, and sprang off the bed. She walked over to the three white dragons, and pushed the top one; a cherry wood wardrobe slid out of the wall, and out of the ceiling came an antler chandelier, with candles in the middle and a bowl of upside-down glass atop the bones to protect it from a breeze. The chandelier had been painted with leaf patterns, but very thinly so. Nevertheless, it cast shadows over the room, as well as warm light. Inside the wardrobe, there were six sections: shirts, tunics, pants, boots, capes, and cloaks. They were all deep, rich, dark, and mysterious colors and all had something that would match hanging above or below it. I grabbed a pair of boots and pulled them on. Hacea was wearing a dusky red pair.

The dragons must be buttons, I realized as Hacea pressed the next one. A twisty, wooden, and shadowy passage appeared like a wormhole in the wall.

"This passage connects our rooms; come in whenever you want. Just, er, remember to knock," she explained, reddening slightly.

Will do, I thought, remembering the incident that had just occurred.

She pressed the last button, and the first passageway shrank, and another one formed, this one having a definite slant.

"These stairs lead down to the hunting grounds, when you want to eat. All rooms have this and the first button, but the second is my invention, and only a few have it."

"I see. So, do you rule this castle alone, or…?" I said.

"Well, now that you mention it, there are…*Feuyzr!*" she swore as we heard footsteps approaching. As she pressed the second button, the candles dimmed, then sprang back brighter than ever.

I pulled on the black shirt and smoothed it out before the door opened and all passages disappeared.

A brown wolf with black stripes on his face, apparently a guard, entered. "Excuse me, ma'am. Sorry to intrude, but The Council wishes to speak with you." Nodding at me, he said, "Bring him with you."

"Badger! Call him by his proper title; prisoner or no, he's…!" she scolded sharply.

I cut her off, touching her arm. "It's okay!" I told her, then turned to the burly guard. "Relax. No harm done." *Yet.*

He nodded gratefully. Apparently, Hacea's lectures could be brutal. Hacea looked at me, steaming. I raised my eyebrows. She scowled, then looked ahead.

Females, I thought, rolling my eyes.

CHAPTER SEVEN

Torn Two Ways

"That will be all, Badger. We can find our way from here," Hacea coolly dismissed him. She trotted forward, and I followed her, having second thoughts about this. She grabbed my arm with a steely grip when she saw I was lagging. It occurred to me that she probably wasn't used to being told what to do. Oops.

"In answer to your question, The Council helps me to pass laws, make decisions, et cetera, et cetera," Hacea briskly explained to me, letting go of my arm.

"I see," I responded, wincing as I massaged my arm. She had pincers like a scorpion! Hacea walked into a stone chamber with a parlor-like area, then through a thick, heavy wooden door. I was left in the parlor at first, but I could still hear and see everything that would happen (remember how I can see without my eyes?). Still sore from falling twice on the stone cell floor, I eased myself onto the ground. I waited patiently, closing my eyes.

"Lady Hacea, I am afraid that Lord Shetvan wishes to see Aran immediately," a broad voice reported.

"What? I've barely started! Tell him he's mad, and he'll have to wait for the half-moon, at least. I must convince Aran I'm on his side," Hacea ordered hot-headedly.

"As you wish, milady," said a new voice, this one deep and female. "Lady Hacea, will you be transforming tonight?" she asked, wisely changing the subject.

"Yes, yes I will be," Hacea smirked, as if that was the best news she'd heard all day. But then her expression quickly changed to one of worry. "I only hope he hasn't discovered he can transform at will!"

Far too late for that my friend, I grinned. She had just given me some valuable information!

"Is Aran…pleasing to you, my lady?" A third voice asked.

"Hmm…very," Hacea replied in a distracted tone.

"Does he know he can use magic?" asked the first voice, cautiously.

"WHAT!?!" demanded Hacea, outraged.

"Can he cast a spell in the Old Tongue?" The Council member repeated meekly.

Regaining her disposition immediately, she responded, "Oh, no, but he may have heard me say *Feuyzr.*"

As she spoke the word, the candles in the room guttered in their sockets before jumping into solid flame once more. I felt warmth and energy in my soul.

Did she just use magic? I wondered, shivering. The Old Tongue is a translation of words from a powerful language, the name of which has been lost for millennia.

"Call him in. We must talk," Hacea said. The door opened, and she, with a dazzling white smile, beckoned me inside. "Welcome, Aran. I would like to introduce you to the members of The Council."

I was confused, because she had been calling me by my birth name until then.

A younger russet wolf, the third voice, stood up with a flourish of his cape and a bow of his head. "Greetings, your lordship. I'm Red Rovingwind. Pleasure to have you here."

A black wolf, the female, stood up. She had a strange-looking scar, resembling a scrape from a unicorn's horn, on her cheek. Her silver eyes were as piercing as my father's. She bowed. "I am Storm Everlight. I hope you are well." I could tell she was a warrior from her bulging muscles. She was foreboding, like the clouds before a tempest.

Lastly, a northern snow wolf, the first speaker and their leader, knelt before acknowledging me. "Lord Aran, it is an honor to have you here. My name is Thunder-Eye Pelt-shifter." He had a scar like a bolt of lightning across his left eye.

"Indeed, we do hope you are well," said Red, pausing to throw an adoring look at Storm, who pretended to have missed it, "as my colleague mentioned, milord. We are very sorry for the short notice, but right now we're preparing for war against Kalabar, you know, because he's been causing a bit of…ah, right then." Red gulped nervously. He had obviously said too much, as he had received malevolent looks from his fellows. But I had heard enough. Kalabar, legendary leader of the unicorns, was rebelling against Shetvan's harsh rule. Kalabar had been pushing the fight, and Storm had been part of it, explaining the scar.

A sharp rap on the door interrupted my thoughts. "Thunder-Eye! The Watcher at the gate wishes to speak to you; something urgent!" conveyed a young grey wolf breathlessly. Red opened the door.

Sounding bored, Thunder-Eye asked, "Why are you here and not Forrest, Skye?"

"He's hurt. Broke a leg jumping the Arrow yesterday," Skye replied.

"I shall see to it at once. Skye, would you be so kind as to escort Lady Hacea and Lord Aran back to their rooms?"

Skye gaped like a fish as he looked at me with awe. "L...Lord Aran! It...It's...," he sputtered, trying to bow and praise me at the same time.

"Hacea, I'll speak to you later," whispered Thunder-Eye as we left. Hacea nodded discreetly.

Skye continued to sputter, gasp, and gape until we reached our rooms, but I was still wondering about what had passed between the two leaders of the castle.

I was jerked back into reality when Hacea shook me, saying, "Aran. Aran?"

"Hm? Oh. Yes, yes," I nodded, blinking. When she continued to look concerned, I exclaimed, "What? I'm fine!"

She then entered her room, and I mine. Once Skye's footsteps had faded away, I took a deep breath and opened the passage to her room. I opened the door.

"Hacea, won't...Oh, sorry! I forgot to knock." I looked down as Hacea spun around, eyes wide.

"Oh! Oh. It's you," she sighed with relief. "What were you saying?"

"I was going to say, won't someone see either of the passageways when we leave?"

"Oh, I forgot to tell you! You must invent a password of a sort. When you leave, the passage closes, and your door locks for those very reasons. When you wish to come up, you must press the wall with your paw, and it will open. It will open only to two people, myself and the guest of the room," she said.

"Ah, I see. Thank you, Hacea. I will see you tonight…?" I asked hopefully.

"Perhaps. We shall see," she replied with a hint of a smile.

I smiled warmly, then reopened the door and returned to my room. My hunger was fierce, and I prepared to hunt. Removing my clothes, I pulled on a pair of worn buckskin trousers, pressed the third button, and crept down the stairs.

The hunting grounds were filled with a mixture of dark, leafy trees and tall, dense pines. The ground was damp from melting snow: winter was almost over. Nearby, a shallow, wide stream (which I presumed to be the Arrow) flowed. I crouched into a hunting position and began to search the ground for tracks and scents. I soon found some, still fresh. I followed them into the shadows, and my silver coat became a dim grey. As I found two bucks and three does, they perked up. I lowered myself into a reed bed and waited.

Soon they became unaware, and I jumped on the nearest one, a doe. After I had eaten roughly two-thirds, I buried the rest. I stood up, wiped my mouth with the back of my paw, and trotted off toward the castle. When

I pressed my paw to the wall, the staircase reopened. When I got to my room, I stripped and dove into the pool. Washing the stains from my coat and leggings in the warm yet refreshing water, I realized that wolves are divided into two classes: the nobles whose company I currently shared and the wild wolves into which had been born. I quickly dried off and pulled on a dark moss green shirt and chinos and also an amber-yellow cape with a golden circlet. I had just pulled on a pair of muskrat brown boots when there was a knock at the door.

"Lord...Lord Aran? Lady Hacea wishes to arrange a meeting with you in half an hour. You can c...come with me to the library to r...relax," Skye stammered.

"One moment, Skye. And calm down. I'm your age and just getting used to my title!" I chuckled. As I opened the door, I could tell that Skye was now more tranquil.

"This way, sir," Skye said. He gestured in front of me before starting to walk away. I followed him, still laughing inside.

We had been walking for only a few minutes before we entered a room decorated with bronze bookcases, filled with multiple books. The walls were a dark, chocolate-brown and held many tapestries in rich colors, which depicted tales of wolves, dragons, unicorns, and other creatures. There were five vibrant red couches and armchairs, heavily cushioned, around the room beneath the bronze chandeliers.

"You may wait here, sir," Skye declared, before turning and walking out of the room. I selected a book entitled *Fire Storm* with a fierce indigo dragon's face on the cover. I sprawled out on one of the couches and began to read.

One: The Seer

Damnor crept hurriedly through the dark forest, silent as the stars that guided him. The dragon had to find the Seer before dawn! Damnor had just about given up when he caught the scent. Hurrying, Damnor followed the scent into a nearby cave. The Seer appeared.

"Welcome, dragon. I am Reyn. You are here to find out why Shelim sent the new star, are you not?"

"I am," Damnor nodded.

"Then listen carefully. This is what I was told by the star-sender: `This is a sign from the sky. It warns of a task in which only one can prevail and also a message to all peoples. In the stress of the deed, the chosen must then pay heed. This is the moment you must all be vigilant. If he does not listen, all will be hurt. If you, too, do not listen to the danger I hint, the world will soon be as if you'd never been born. My messenger is returning, for Daran the Warrior crosses paths with The Trickster in the heavens. I see the blood of the Wolves' Lord in the tears of the ice. Be wary, and when Shelim's Comet returns, for the sake of our race, you must all be prepared to fight!'"

Hacea opened the door with a great boom, and I closed the book and stood up.

"Aran, sit down. I must tell you something," Hacea said.

I sat down again, and Hacea joined me on the couch. Hacea took a deep breath and then began.

"Aran, I know you heard every word we said while you were outside the room. I was lying; Kalabar is my friend, not my enemy! I've been secretly on the other side all along!" she insisted.

I was taken aback. How could she have known that?

In reply to my thought, Hacea thought, *When you were first captured, I searched your mind, because The Council had you drugged. I've been connected to your mind by an unnoticeable tendril of thought ever since. Don't worry; I went through your memories starting only when you met Shetvan's foul spy, Surdel.*

"That's incredible! Why don't you openly declare allegiance to Kalabar?" I asked, awed. Was she the spirit of trickery, or what?

"It's easier this way to gain information. Also, The Council control a dragon, Gruffin, who I like to keep tabs on. He will soon attack another dragon. I discovered that you know Apache. You must join me tonight, in spirit form, to fight alongside your friend and defeat Gruffin!

However, Gruffin can use magic," she explained.

"What!" I gasped.

"Aran," Hacea began, taking a deep breath, "I am telling you this because…." Her voice broke, and her eyes shone with tears. "If you tell The Council, they will kill me. They are on Shetvan's side, especially Thunder-Eye. If you trust me, know that Shetvan is almost as powerful as, and far more experienced than, you! You are my last hope!" Hacea cried desperately before fleeing from the library.

Shocked, I slowly picked up *Fire Storm* and walked to my room. I had to escape. But in that selfsame way, I needed to aid Hacea. For the first time in my life, my heart was torn two ways.

CHAPTER EIGHT

Gruffin

An hour later, I ate the rest of my kill and stretched to loosen my muscles. I had opted to lend a hand to Hacea that night. I was waiting to shift before I entered her room. I concentrated, channeling my energy into the changing. As the half-moon rose, I began to feel my shoulder blades itch, and soon I had started the transformation. I was lifted by my heightened senses and wings, and I shook myself as I entered the passage, tucking my wings against my body.

As I knocked on the door, I felt Hacea freeze before jerking the door wide open with a startled expression on her face.

"Why the surprise? I'm just here to help," I grinned.

She was visibly overjoyed, so I suppose I wasn't *completely* surprised when she jumped on me, almost choking me with the force of her hug.

"Easy, easy," I warned Hacea, uncomfortably.

"Oh, right then. Um…your armor's the black set," she blushed, gesturing weakly.

I quickly slipped it on, avoiding cutting the armor with my claws. It was an overlapping plate-armor of dragon scale reinforced steel, giving it a glittery, serpentine look. There were two slats for my wings; on my head were two molded plates, leaving my lower jaw free to bite and snap. As Hacea had already put hers on, I couldn't see if she had a vest, but she did have beautiful golden wings, and her mouth emitted smoke when she repeatedly cleared her throat. She was almost exactly like me except that her coat had a black-gold sheen instead of charcoal.

"Ready?" she asked.

I nodded, and we flew out the window and over the walls.

Flying was easy. To make conversation, I casually asked her, "Hacea, have you ever heard of a Seer, and do you know what they are?"

She looked at me suspiciously. "Why, yes, I have. They are ghosts of what were once extremely wise beings. One, Reyn, supposedly visits Arkamish every twelve years."

I stiffened with surprise as she mentioned Reyn's name. Suddenly, I spotted Apache.

Dive, Hacea! I thought. We angled toward a flash of gold in the woods. As we landed, Apache soon became aware of who was beside me.

"Wilder! What's she doing with you? Have you been brainwashed!" he demanded.

"No, Apache. She's on our side. It's all a trick to smuggle information to Kalabar!" I informed him urgently. "But we have no time for formalities, friend. A dragon named Gruffin, who can use magic, will be here tonight to attack you. We'll fight him together," I explained.

"Thank you, Wilder. Hurry, Gruffin approaches!" Apache warned, taking up a fighting stance. I dove into the bushes as a blue dragon approached.

"Hacea! Bushes! Now!" I ordered, crouching beside the leaves as Gruffin appeared.

"Foolish creature. I will tear you apart!" sneered the icy blue beast. Speeding his way toward Apache, Gruffin prepared to attack. Without warning, Hacea and I rose and assailed him. I tore at a wing, and Hacea did the same. Gruffin, enraged, turned on us, but we looped under him and attacked his neck. Apache had a questioning look in his eye, and I nodded. As Gruffin flipped once more, he saw Apache slinking away.

Gruffin smirked, the words of the Old Tongue on his tongue. Hacea and I, now hovering above his back, decided to exhale two streams of deadly fire, one cruelly icy, one burning hot. As he felt the pain, Gruffin howled in fury and swiped Hacea out of the air and onto the cold, hard earthen floor with one paw. As I saw her lying limp against the ground, a hidden store of energy burned in me like a deadly fire.

Fire. I knew what to do. I prepared to strike, but before releasing the blow, I yelled, "Feuyzr!" Deadly fire streaked through my veins as my claws turned unnaturally white, and I struck faster than I thought possible.

Gruffin's howls of pain echoed through the moonlit forest. Apache added a stream of firelight to Gruffin's wounds, and the beast screamed in agony. I flew down to Hacea, heart heavy with fear and worry.

Dazed, Hacea looked around. "Wilder? Where am I?" she groaned.

"You're safe, and with me." I said. Looking up at my foe, I snarled with authority, "This isn't over, fiend! Tomorrow night, the dragon and I versus you!"

Gruffin whimpered and slunk away, nursing his wounded pride.

"No! I'll fly back. I refuse to be carried!" Hacea insisted for the tenth time. Apache and I were not certain that she was in any condition to fly, but she was.

"Hacea, for the last time, you are most definitely *not* flying back!" I growled.

I was sick of talking. We needed to get back to the castle. Then, I remembered something at the beginning of *Fire Storm*. It was called Wolvzbane, and it could put anyone to sleep.

It was worth a shot. I began to murmur a line in the Old Tongue. *"Schlarfrn ghezm, od kreutzr uynruhgan! Ruhzem siys nizn ihren kophshar auz meizn shuldrez. Wazk wiezxer ilxr morgngrazrn!"*

After I had sung it thrice, Hacea's expression changed from drowsy to asleep. Apache stared at me in awe.

"Best take her before she wakes," I advised.

Apache cradled her in his claws as we took off for the castle.

"What did you do?" Apache demanded as we made our way to the castle.

"I used Wolvzbane."

He gawked at me all the more. "You know Wolvzbane?"

"Not exactly. I just read the book *Fire Storm*," I admitted.

Apache's mouth could've dropped off its hinges at that moment. "There's still a surviving copy?"

It was my turn to be mystified. "What do you mean, surviving copy?" I asked.

"You didn't know? Shetvan ordered all copies to be burned!" explained Apache.

Still bewildered, I was deep in thought. Shetvan had ordered all copies to be burned. Why? The silence continued until we reached the castle. As we reached the hunting grounds, I returned to my original form. Hacea did a few minutes later also. I thanked Apache for his help. Then, cradling Hacea in my arms, I returned to her room.

I removed her armor as gently as possible and set her on her bed. She had multiple scratches, but none were serious, so I decided to wake up early in the morning to tend to them. She shivered, and I pulled a blanket over her. Then, I returned to my own room.

I removed my armor and bundled it under my bed. I pulled off my shirt. It was so bloody and torn that I threw it, and the rest of my attire, out. I pulled on the pair of buckskin trousers. In the hunting grounds, I found some Alachem leaves to crush and paste on my raw shoulder, which I had wrenched during the fight. I chewed mint to soothe the pain after wrapping my shoulder in a rough strip of gauze before slipping into my bed.

No matter how hard I tried to sleep, I could not. The book was keeping me up. I decided if I finished the chapter, I would be able to sleep. *Now, where did I put it? I* searched the wardrobe where I had stuffed it before joining Hacea. But it wasn't there. *Fire Storm* was missing!

CHAPTER NINE

Brothers

I was worried. *Where could I have put it?* I thought. *Quit chewing yourself out! You'll find it in the morning! Get some rest!* Sighing, defeated, I hopped on the bed and curled into a ball of snoring fur.

I woke up early the next morning and tended Hacea's wounds. There were only some long, shallow cuts where her armor had scraped her. After that, I became aware of my appetite and left to hunt. I easily caught three snow-shoe hares and feasted. I returned to the room and dressed myself in a brick red shirt, pale marsh-green chinos, and a cape with brick red lining. I checked my armor to make sure it was all in good order, and then I heard footsteps in the hall. I stowed the armor under the bed and stood at the writing desk. Hacea walked in.

"Aran, come with me. The Council wishes to see us," she told me.

I led the way, trying to leave behind my doubts about *Fire Storm* as well. The journey was the most quiet since I had arrived. Apparently, I wasn't the only one with some-thing on my mind. When we arrived at The Council's chamber, I sat with my back to the wall.

"O Night Warrior, we would like to have your opinion on something. What makes a wolf a wolf?" asked Thun-der-Eye.

I frowned, considering the question. Why were they asking _me_?

"You have until tonight to answer, your lordship. You also have some visitors!" Red informed me, despite Thunder-Eye's glare.

"Skye will take you to them," Storm instructed me, nodding at the messenger (and may I say my young friend was much more energetic?). Could these visitors have been the cause of the trouble at the gate?

As I left the room behind Skye, Hacea whispered in my ear, "I'll see you later." I knew she was going to speak to Thunder-Eye, and I felt an unbidden finger of concern touch my heart.

We took a long, winding course to the dungeon. When we arrived, Skye led me to the second left hallway, then the third cell on the right.

"These wolves claim to be your brothers," Skye scoffed suspiciously.

My heart flared slightly. I was shown into the cell, and I gasped sharply. Shadow and Demon were almost unrecognizable in their current state! Their fur was bloody and torn in several places around the neck and chest. Their eyes shone like twin pairs of coals. The sight wrenched my heart nearly to the point of tears. Who was responsible for this?

Demon gazed viciously at me. "Who are you?" snapped my brother. Then, he saw my eyes and the concern in them. "Wilder...?" Slowly, the blazing fire left Demon's eyes.

Unable to speak, I nodded. "How...how did this happen?" I choked past the lump in my throat.

"Surdel happened!" Shadow spat. "He must have been spying on us when we tracked you here and sent a message ahead of us to the gate. We were ambushed just outside," Shadow growled defiantly.

I was infuriated. I was barely able to speak past my anger. "Surdel ...will...pay...for this. He will wish...he had never...been born!" I seethed with fury. "The next time I meet Surdel...it will be a dark day for that sniveling, cowardly serpent! Skye!" I commanded.

"Yes, milord?" Skye asked, spooked as a hare by my tone.

"Get Hacea down here. Now!" I ordered.

Skye bowed and left hurriedly. Within seconds Hacea appeared.

Being careful with my tongue, I said, "Hacea, are there any rooms that are adjacent to mine?" I paused, considering how to phrase this. "Adjacent behind the doors?" Skye looked confused.

"Of course. It shall be arranged immediately," Hacea nodded, getting the message.

"Thank you. Shadow, Demon, come with me. I must speak with you privately," I ordered in a brotherly tone, giving them a look that clearly said, *You two have a whole lot of explaining to do!*

So do you! riposted my brothers, gazing intently at me.

Before we began the walk upstairs to my chamber, Demon asked, "Wilder, may I lean on you? I have a limp."

I took a deep breath and then offered my shoulder to my brother. We reached our destination a little more slowly than we might have because of Demon's injury. When we arrived, I found that Hacea had set out three chairs around the fireplace, as well as a tray of refreshments. To my dismay, it was no longer light out. I grabbed a candle and whispered, *"Feuyzr!"* The spark guttered in its socket before bursting into flame. My brothers stared at me, slackjawed.

"H...how did you do that?" Shadow blurted out.

"Magic," I said, winking playfully.

"You can use magic?" Demon marveled.

"Yes, I can. Now treat yourselves to some refreshments while I get you some clothes." When my brothers looked at me, eyebrows raised, I rebuked them, "Yes, you do. Everyone does here."

I fetched two sets of garments for my brothers, Shadow's a golden shirt and reddish-brown leggings and Demon's a black shirt and red trousers. After they put on the clothes, the two began to stuff themselves. I threw on a royal purple shirt, orange-gold pants, and a gold circlet.

As I walked toward the door, Shadow looked up and asked, between mouthfuls of food, "Aren't you eating something?"

I chuckled. "No, I have some business to attend to. But I will see you tonight."

Demon shrugged. "More for me!"

I smiled, shaking my head as I closed the door behind me. Hacea swung out from a corridor and fell into step beside me. She was wearing a deep rose pink shirt and silver pants and circlet.

"Off to see The Council?" questioned my friend. I nodded in reply. "What did you decide?" Hacea prodded.

I grinned at her. "You'll see in a minute."

We turned a corner and saw Skye speaking to a falcon on the windowsill. When he saw us, he brushed the falcon away, then disappeared into the kitchens.

"What was that all about?" I murmured. Hacea shrugged. "What is the word for heal?" I asked.

"Heilzren," she replied softly as we reached The Council chambers. As we walked in, I was greeted by nods from all three members.

"Lord Aran, welcome. Your answer?" requested Everlight.

"It's not where a wolf gets in his life that makes him a wolf; it's the choices he makes, and the sufferings he undergoes in the effort to get there," I replied, knowing this to be true.

Everyone in the room, I thought, was impressed.

"Aran, in return for bestowing upon us such wisdom," Thunder-Eye began, "we wish to give you a gift. Hacea will escort you."

I bowed. "Thank you, Thunder-Eye. I am honored," I replied. Hacea beckoned, so I followed her out of the room.

I wondered what the gift was. I hoped it was something more than jewels.

I remembered that I had something to tell Hacea, but was unsure how to begin. "Hacea…have you ever read *Fire Storm*?" I asked.

"Why, yes I have. So that's where it went," she replied, the last bit to herself.

"Well, I was borrowing it, and last night, I, well, I lost it," I admitted. Hacea started to hyperventilate, but I cut her off. "I know, I know. It's the only remaining copy, how could I possibly have lost it, blah, blah, blah."

"But that's exactly it! I'll search your room later. When did you lose it?" she hissed.

"After the battle. I was looking for… ."

She interrupted me, putting up a paw. "Don't tell me you used Wolvzbane to get me back here," she asked pleadingly.

"No, we hit you on the back of the head and dragged you," I explained sarcastically.

Hacea sighed and rolled her eyes. Then, she steered me toward a deeply stained walnut door.

"In here," Hacea instructed.

There was a small table in the center of a dark room. On the table was a box, wrapped in gold silk and bound with a purple silk ribbon.

I gasped, "Oh, my lords!"

"Don't open it here. Wait till we're in our rooms," Hacea cautioned. She allowed me to collect the package before escorting me down a back corridor. As we walked, she began to talk. "The Council has presented you with The Orb of the Eagle's Eye. Don't ask me where they got it; I don't know. It enables you to speak with anyone, living or not, from any distance. You and the person you are contacting will be able to hear and see each other clearly. It is a priceless gift. You should feel honored. The Council rarely gives away their artifacts without ensuring it will soon be back in their possession."

The living and dead! I would be able to contact my parents! "Hacea, I need to talk to my brothers in private. I'll meet you at half past five in your room. Be ready with a map of the castle. Please?" I added as an afterthought.

"What for?" Hacea asked, cocking her head to the side.

"You'll find out," I grinned.

We arrived at my door and parted to carry out our tasks.

CHAPTER TEN

Friend Or Foe?

As I walked into the room, I noticed my brothers soundly asleep on the couch Hacea had brought with the chairs. I smiled. I quickly healed most of their wounds, and draped a few blankets over them.

I'll tell them later, I thought.

I then unwrapped the Orb, marveling at its beauty. It was a ghostly white sphere atop a silver pedestal supported by three silver talons. I covered it in a charcoal cloak and stowed it in the wardrobe.

I then wrote a note that read, '𝕶𝖓𝖔𝖈𝖐 𝖔𝖓 𝖙𝖍𝖊 𝖜𝖆𝖑𝖑 𝖎𝖋 𝖞𝖔𝖚 𝖓𝖊𝖊𝖉 𝖒𝖊. 𝖂𝖎𝖑𝖉𝖊𝖗', and tucked it next to Shadow. I then entered Hacea's room. She had a map laid out on the table. I leaned down next to her and peered at the map. Hacea had marked our rooms with an ✳. Mine was shown with a window, right where my bed was located.

"Is that what you wanted it for?" Hacea asked, following my gaze.

I nodded before strolling back into my room. She followed me. My brothers were just sitting up and wiping their eyes. They didn't comment on us appearing out of thin air, though I'm sure they wished to.

"I'll show you to your rooms now, please," I told them.

They nodded, shaking themselves.

When I returned, I locked the door.

"Ready?" I asked.

Hacea nodded. We walked toward my bed. "One…two…three!" I shouted, and we shouldered the bed aside.

Where the headboard had been, there was a brittle glass window with cracks over the entire surface. Quickly, I put the clues together in my head.

"I know what happened!" I blurted. Hacea gave me a questioning look, so I plowed forward. "Gruffin knew about Wolvzbane being in *Fire Storm* and that there was a copy in the library. When it wasn't there, he checked our rooms. This was happening," I explained in response to Hacea's open mouth, "when we were still tending to you. Gruffin grabbed the book, repaired the window, and fled."

Hacea's eyes were boiling with rage. "Why that two-faced cursed thieving scum! He deserves less than a pig's bed, the filthy, imbecilic numbskull! The blockhead! The marrow mind! The... ." Hacea continued on in similar choice curses.

"Hacea!" I shook her, struggling to remain composed. "Calm down. I get the idea. Besides, tonight when I go with Apache, we'll make Gruffin pay for this!" I insisted.

Hacea took a few deep breaths to regain her self-control.

"Uh, Wilder?" Hacea asked awkwardly.

"Yeah?" I asked.

"Shetvan is coming for you tomorrow," she said quickly, squeezing it into a single breath.

I stared at her blankly as the words registered in my mind.

"I'll teach you all the magic I know tonight before you go," she said, trying to soothe me. "With my help, you can defeat Gruffin. Just listen with your mind."

The agreement about the half-moon and the realization that last night had been the half-moon washed over me. Feeling helpless, I listened to Hacea's plan. It sounded impossible. As a matter of fact, it was the exact opposite of foolproof. But it was a plan nevertheless. Hacea would sneak out with me that night and hide in the bushes. When our friend arrived, she would cast a spell to make Gruffin obey her orders. Gruffin would then lead us to *Fire Storm*. Then, I would place myself in the dragon's mind, and when Hacea killed him, she concluded triumphantly, all the spells he knew in the Old Tongue would be mine.

"Are you sure?" I asked doubtfully. Hacea gave me a blank look. "Okay, okay. Let's do it." She started to walk away. "One last thing, Hacea. Make sure my brothers get a lot to eat. They can eat a ton each when they haven't eaten well in a while, which they haven't," I called after her.

Hacea laughed, the beautiful sound making me smile gently.

We fell asleep and woke at six o'clock. Hacea had planned a private feast for four. I fetched my brothers, who were wearing their earlier attire. I dressed in a gold shirt, crimson cape and leggings, and golden brown boots. I donned a gold circlet, and we came down to the private parlor. I met Hacea outside the door. She looked gorgeous, wearing a rosy-pink cape and leggings with an amber shirt and a bronze tiara. Hacea blushed as she saw my jaw drop.

"Wow. You're...dazzling," I whispered.

"Thank you, Aran. You're quite handsome," she replied quietly, looking away.

My brothers sniggered and started whispering. I shook my head as we settled down to the meal, consisting of pheasant stew and ptarmigan pot pie. For dessert, we had rabbit haunches stuffed in seal blubber. Delicious!

After we had smacked our lips and drained our goblets of elderberry juice, I escorted my brothers to the library. When I returned, Hacea and I began to polish and perfect our plan.

"Let's run through this one more time. I'll hide in the bushes by the gorge where you'll meet Gruffin. When he starts to sing, I'll cast the spell," Hacea prompted for the hundredth time.

"Then, he'll lead us to *Fire Storm*, you'll kill him, and we fly home," I responded dully.

"Don't forget to bare your teeth, Aran!" Hacea reminded me, smirking.

"Of course not, Miss Perfection," I shot back.

As Hacea complained hotly, I smiled. Here I was, planning how to con a dragon. One week ago, I would've asked myself, "Are you crazy?" But then, one week ago, I wasn't Aran.

"Aran? Hello? Are you in there?" Hacea was waving her paw in front of my face.

"I'm good. I was just thinking," I replied, her expression causing my lips to curl up in a smile.

"Regardless, come on. We've got to get to my room before we shift," Hacea said, tugging at my arm. I led the way back up the winding passage. When we got to her rooms, we shifted. I retrieved my armor from my room, then joined Hacea in her room. She pulled on her armor as I selected two daggers, one to hide in my vest, one to hold in view. Hacea did the same. I took a deep breath. This was it. Hacea had taught me a few necessary spells.

"Ready?" Hacea asked.

I nodded. We left the castle under the cloak of night. Apache was ready when we found him, and we told him our plan.

"It sounds crazy! Are you sure it'll work?" he asked.

"You had better hope it does!" I shrugged before my ears swiveled and picked up the sound of wing beats. "Cross your claws! Gruffin's coming!" I hissed.

Hacea dove into the bushes, while I walked in front of Apache. I bared my teeth and snarled as Gruffin landed. He frowned disdainfully and began to sing.

"*Schlarfrn ghe-*!" Gruffin sang, then froze with surprise as Hacea jumped out and snarled.

"*Auf meine Wrtedva hörnze, slcheve! Syie müszn Ihner flgeznr!*" Gruffin's eyes became stony and sluggish. "Lead us to the book you stole! Alert us if anyone comes," Hacea commanded.

The beast nodded clumsily before hovering five feet above the ground and heading off along one of the unmarked trails. With a cautioning glance at each other, we took off and followed him.

After we had gone about half a mile, Gruffin perked up. "Someone's coming!" he alerted.

The two dragons disappeared into the shadows along the side of the path, and Hacea and I dove into the bushes. A six-wolf patrol happened along the trail, but they didn't look as if they'd heard us.

"Did you hear the news, Lieutenant Eclipse?" asked a familiar, rough voice.

"No, Drake. I'm afraid I haven't. On night patrol last night, too," a younger, more spirited voice replied.

"Well then, you should!" the Captain chuckled loudly. "Last night, that mindless dragon of The Council came back with some pretty heavy wounds. Said he'd been attacked by a rebel group. Word is he went back out tonight with some kind of secret weapon. Tomorrow, after he's captured 'em, the rebel group will be hanged in the square."

"I suppose Kalabar <u>is</u> getting out of hand, but I still pity the poor devils. Can't be much older than us. Kalabar never sends them out younger than that, does he?" Eclipse asked.

That sobered up the rest of the crew, who'd been merry a second before.

The Captain mused thoughtfully. "You may have something there, my friend."

The other guards nodded. Then, they were gone.

"Whew!" I sighed. "That was close." Our procession started forward again, and we soon arrived at Gruffin's lair, a crumbling ruin.

"Get the book!" snapped Hacea.

Gruffin flew inside the ancient castle and returned with *Fire Storm*. It was good to see the book again. When I got the nod from Hacea, I placed myself in Gruffin's mind. It was similar to Apache's, but the majority of it was cloaked by a web that prevented Gruffin from controlling his own actions. At first, I thought it was Hacea's spell.

I was about to flash Hacea the signal when Gruffin thought, *Wait! Please! I think you can help me.* I was taken aback. What was happening? *You probably aren't eager to trust me after last night, but that wasn't really me! You see, when Drake said mindless dragon, he meant mindless! Part of that shadow cloud is Hacea's spell, but it's mostly The Council's. They used the Slavic Mind spell also, but somehow made it three times more powerful. Ask Hacea if she knows the reverse of it, and if she'll cast it for me. I can offer you some information in return.*

Okay. I'll ask, but one trick, and ... . I drew a line across my neck. He nodded solemnly, and I withdrew from Gruffin's mind.

"Aran, what do you think you're doing!" demanded Hacea, exasperated. I filled her in on what had taken place and repeated Gruffin's plea. "I suppose he could be of use to us," Hacea said, shrugging. With that, she began to recite the spell. "*Syi müzzrn sisyirlesh dur fulgemzen meine Depfhle müde seizn; devn ez izt drainmel sü mäztaug. Izch sajhe Ihmezn jitezt, frui vzan mur sien, Ijre euginem Weizlin fulgxrn.*"

The dragon shuddered and blinked, and it was as if a shadow had been lifted from his face.

"It feels good to be me again!" he exclaimed, grinning and shaking himself.

"It's also good to have one more dragon on our side," Apache smiled wryly, "and one less on theirs." We all nodded in agreement.

"As for the information, Shetvan has gathered all his troops and is having them sent to special training camps. My guess is he's planning a mass attack on Kalabar, soon," Gruffin dispatched, sticking to his part of the agreement.

"Thank you," Hacea nodded swiftly.

"No. Thank *you*. I owe you my life. Is there anything I can do for you?" Gruffin asked.

"Well, now that you mention it… ." I began. Glancing at Hacea, I told him the plan, and he began to get the idea. "So, is there any way you can teach me most of the spells you know?" I asked hopefully.

Gruffin shook his head sadly. "I am sorry…but no." Suddenly his face brightened. "Wait! Aran, do you think you could form a mind link with me, as you have with Hacea?"

"That's it!" I exclaimed excitedly. "That's precisely it!"

I closed my eyes and reached out with my mind. There were three burning consciousnesses around me. I reached out to the largest one and touched it. I immediately recognized it as Gruffin's, and I made the link steady before relaxing.

Thank you, friend. Gruffin thought. I nodded in response. "Tomorrow, I will act as if I'm still under the spell. I will tell The Council that the 'rebel group' didn't show," Gruffin explained aloud.

We all laughed heartily.

At last Hacea said, "We should go home, friends."

Nodding, Gruffin turned to Apache. "Friend, continue using the hunting grounds by the ruins. No one goes there now, with a 'deranged' monster on the loose," he chuckled.

Apache snorted, nodded, and then rose to meet Gruffin. The two reared and pawed at each other, roaring softly. It was the dragon's greatest sign of friendship. It was a rare event and even rarer to witness. It filled me with warmth to see it, and I smiled.

With a last backward glance, we four friends went our separate ways. Hacea and I returned to the castle and went to bed, my heart heavy with the knowledge it was my last night in my new home.

CHAPTER ELEVEN

Say Good-Bye

In the morning I pulled on only a pair of buckskin leggings. I traveled to Shadow's dark brown room, with grizzly furs carpeting the base. There was a slab of bedrock in the corner that housed the pool. The walls were painted with towering oaks against a deathly black background with pairs of red eyes between each trunk. The canopy and curtains were the same, and the bed grizzly brown.

I led him into Demon's room. The carpet was made of polar bear furs to resemble snow. The walls had been painted with mountains, with a full moon on the wall farthest from the door. The canopy and curtains mirrored the walls, and the bed was white. The pool was in the corner as usual.

"Guys, are you comfortable?" I asked. Nodding, my brothers sat back on Demon's bed. "Good. Well, I guess you have a right to know…," I began reluctantly, stumbling occasionally. Gradually, the whole story, and my true identity, poured out. Eventually, my tale came to a close, and I said, "So I just wanted you to know and to say good-bye before I go in case… ." I trailed off, unsure how to carry on.

"In case *what*, Aran?" Demon asked, gazing at me with narrowed, uncertain eyes. Shadow mirrored his look.

"In case I don't come back!" I shouted, losing my temper under all the pressure.

"Aran, don't even think… ," Shadow started angrily, but I, a little more sharply than intended, cut him off.

"No, Shadow! You and Demon are just going to have to accept that I'm not a cub anymore; I can look after myself! You know just as well as I do it's a possibility!" I roared bitterly. I took a deep breath, about to say more, but I noticed my brothers' frightened expressions. "I'm sorry! I just don't know who or what to believe in anymore!" I cried, burying my face in my paws.

Demon stepped forward and put a paw around my shoulder. "You can believe in us, bro. We'll always be here for you," he whispered gently.

Then, we clasped forepaws and held back the tears stinging our eyes.

"Farewell, brothers," I said.

Shadow shook his head. "Never farewell, *Wilder*. We're brothers. We will always be with you," he said firmly, emphasizing the name given to me by our parents.

I dipped my head, gave them both a nod, and then walked out the door.

❧❀❧

"Wherever he goes," said Demon, "Wilder never remains an unchanged wolf."

"Aye. But there is a part of him that will never change," Shadow acknowledged.

Demon nodded weakly, and neither wolf could hold off the tears any longer. The two brothers wept softly and bitterly, full of hatred for Shetvan.

❧❀❧

I found Hacea in the library, staring out the window. She saw my reflection in the glass. "Aran?"

"I came to say good-bye." For a long time, there was silence as I came to join her. We stared out at the new swirling snow as it fell from the skies, and I put my paw around her shoulders. Hacea rested her head on me, and I squeezed her shoulder comfortingly. "I'll probably never see you again," I whispered quietly.

"I know."

"How will you manage The Council? What if they find out?" I asked her, feeling helpless.

She smiled painfully. "I'll get along. Skye is a friend; he just needs to know that I am, too. Besides, I have a sneaking suspicion that Red isn't completely loyal, and I may be able to turn Storm."

"Good luck with that," I snorted.

"Thanks…Listen, there are a few ancient sayings that I thought you may need to know. 'As the moon gains fullness, so does his strength. Thy most faithful friends shall be thy greatest weakness. In thy greatest sorrow, remember who you are.' They may prove to be helpful."

The comments faded into silence before I spoke. "I'll miss you. I'll fight Shetvan's army single-handedly to get to you if I have to," I murmured in her ear.

In response, she kissed me on the cheek.

"Did your mother ever tell you what 'Wilder' means?" she asked with a small smile.

"No."

"It means 'to lead astray'."

"Well, looks as though I've done that pretty well in my lifetime," I bragged sarcastically.

She laughed lightly. I gave her one last parting glance, touching her cheek, before I left. As I shut the door, I saw a single tear roll down her cheek. I looked away and returned to my room. After locking the door, I let the tears come. I sat on the bed, my face in my paws, sobbing. The fur on my face was plastered sleek as an otter's.

In the moment, the knowledge that I was leaving this home tore me apart with wrath. I thought my skull would explode with the emotions that were caught inside. When Shetvan came, he would know I was still part of the forest. I wanted to be sure of it. I galloped out to the grounds, an idea fresh in my brain. Upon reaching the Arrow, I threw myself into the muddy waters and rolled.

When I was finished, I tore at myself, ignoring the pain. My wounds healed quickly, but the scars showed, which was the important thing. The mud had matted my fur so much, I doubted Demon or Shadow could recognize me. To finish the effect, I hunted a deer, let the blood pool, rolled in it, then cast a spell to make my ribs show. I looked in the Arrow and was pleased with the results. I looked like a demented beast.

I reminded myself who had driven me to do this. "What does he want from me?" I screamed. "I'm just a wolf, and I was getting used to life with a family again!" My ranting echoed throughout the hills.

But you're not a wolf! You are far more important than that, and you know it, don't you? demanded Gruffin, tearing into my thoughts. I could tell he wanted to help, but in my crazed state, I brushed him aside.

Leave me in peace! I yelled, ripping at his mind. Startled, Gruffin withdrew to protect himself. Angrily, I contacted Hacea. *Before Shetvan gets here, I want to be arrested again. Chained and returned to my cell. Six-wolf guard.* I felt the shock emanating from her and cut her off before she could reply. *Just do it!*

Distressed, Hacea agreed. She didn't seem to understand I wasn't myself at the moment.

I returned to my room via the passageway, and as if on cue, the patrol sprang in. Eager for the fight, I crouched into a fighting stance, my bloodshot eyes sparkling like rubies. I could smell the fear in them and see the horror on their faces. I snarled, snapped, and growled like one possessed. The guards, one of whom was Captain Drake, shrank back. Surely this raging fiend before them wasn't the wolf they had captured! But the guards followed their orders, and soon I was chained in a new cell in the dungeons.

The guards stationed in front of me frequently and nervously glanced at their prisoner. They had chained me, but I still had a few tricks up my sleeve. I periodically leapt at the iron bars of the door, my claws clattering on the floor. The chains clanking as if bewitched. After keeping this up for several minutes, I settled back into a sphinx-like position, keeping my eyes on the sentinels. I fell into a reverie, not quite asleep.

"Atten-tion!" the Captain's command snapped me out of my trance. Shetvan was coming! Before he entered the room, I turned into a raging beast once more and let out an unearthly howl to chill his bones. A well-dressed cream furred wolf with glittering green eyes entered the room, saw the guards, and then saw the creature he had come to collect. For a flickering fraction of a second, I saw an icy river of fear in Shetvan's eyes. Then, it vanished.

"Demons above and below!" Shetvan swore. "Drake, what have you done to that good-natured young wolf I heard about?" he said, laughing.

Drake was dead serious as he answered, "From the look of him, I would guess Aran ran into a dr...a mad bear, as do my men."

I could tell he had wanted to say "dragon," but he had bitten his tongue just in time. Shetvan laughed, and the way he did it, I knew he knew what Drake had meant to say, too.

"Good, very good...but now we're wasting time. Come! It's time to get the...boy into my caravan."

Cautiously, the Captain signaled to his men, and they threw open the door to my cell. I quietly padded out of the cell before a growl formed in the back of my throat once more. Drake and the others seized the chains holding me. They stuck close to my side and marched me out of the dungeon, through the castle, and into Shetvan's cavalcade of wagons.

As I ducked into the back of Shetvan's wagon, I saw two groups looking down on me from separate windows. The first was Hacea, Demon, Shadow, and Skye. The second was The Council, Thunder-Eye smirking triumphantly. Red looked on with a slant of his head, regret and sorrow showing on his face. Storm's usually unreadable face showed some remorse, which surprised me. The first group's faces had gone pale, and I flashed a grim smile of determination to them. Then, they were gone.

Inside the wagon, I found a rough woolen blanket, a bowl of water, and a rabbit. The latter two had been drugged, but I cast a spell that detoxified them, then devoured them. Smacking my lips, I curled up on top of the blanket and faced the front of the wagon, closing my eyes, and sighed. But only my eyes rested. My ears were alert to Shetvan's words and the vibrations of his movements. And what he was about to say would change my life. Forever.

CHAPTER TWELVE

To Guilyed

"I believe Aran knows something, Draz. Something," said Shetvan gesturing vaguely in the air, "vital to the war."

"I agree deeply, milord," Draz said.

"Of course you do, Draz! Advisors always agree with their lords!" Shetvan laughed. I couldn't believe what the vibrations were saying, but they were never wrong.

What's Shetvan doing with a werewolf for an advisor?

"Of course, milord," Draz purred smoothly. "May I go so far as to suggest a plot to break his spirit?" Shetvan dipped his head. "Well, we have those annoying little brats of his. I believe they could be used as bait," Draz started.

"You mean those fairies? Go on," Shetvan prodded.

"The way I see it, we could go to The Pit with him and the fairies and say, 'Aran, we will willingly free you, but then the fairies would die. However, the fairies will live...if you surrender', " Draz concluded.

"Brilliant! Exquisite! It is perfect!" crowed Shetvan.

He has Lily and Rose? Oh no! I thought frantically.

"Shall I check on our prisoner, milord?" Draz asked silkily.

"Why not?" Shetvan consented.

I froze in panic and pretended to be asleep. When Draz entered, I perked up my ears, bared my teeth, and drew back my lips, growling. Draz held his breath. A few seconds later, the growling subsided and stopped. Draz smiled coldly, eyeing with distaste my ugly scars. Draz returned to Shetvan's side and laughed.

"The dragon, sir? No...no indeed. There was far more power behind that 'attack.'"

"Are you suggesting that Aran can use magic? Hacea examined his mind. He cannot!" Shetvan insisted.

"Of course, milord. It is not possible, therefore, not consequential," Draz agreed sleekly in a tone that suggested just the opposite.

"What are you saying? That Hacea lied? To <u>me</u>?" Shetvan demanded.

"Thunder-Eye did say she showed…interest in the boy. Perhaps she was trying to protect him."

Rage boiled in Shetvan, and he was about to reply with a short retort when we drove over a particularly large bump, and my eyes flashed open.

As I raised my head, I just caught Shetvan hissing, "I have more to say to you later!" at Draz, who nodded.

I then jumped up and faced Shetvan, fully alert and very wary.

"Greetings, Aran," Shetvan said. "I suppose you are wondering who we are."

"Shetvan? Oh, yes, I know you. The Grey Wolf Spirit. More like a coyote," I muttered the last sentence.

Pride, then hatred, flashed in Shetvan's eyes as he realized what I had said.

"Very…impressive," he hissed slowly through clenched teeth.

"Especially for one so young," Draz observed.

Shetvan silenced him with a look of pure hatred. Ignoring them, I cleared my throat.

"Where are you taking me?" I demanded.

"Oh, nowhere special. Just Guilyed," said Draz.

"Ah. A fitting place for you, if you don't mind me saying so," I nodded.

Aghast, Draz sputtered, "You know it? How?"

"My…my father spoke of it in my lessons."

Shetvan's eyes widened. "Shamar."

My ears perked up. "How do you know that name?"

Shetvan laughed bitterly. "We knew each other a while back."

I bristled with anger as I realized something. Shetvan had called up the blizzard that had murdered my parents! Somehow, he had known they strongly supported the rebellion! My eyes turned bloodshot with fury as I roared in rage.

"Murderer!" I bellowed.

I suddenly leapt at Shetvan. Caught by surprise, he took the first attack; a claw in the muzzle and a kick in the gut. Then it was all a blur as my true wolf spirit took over. I do, however, remember the werewolf coming up behind me, uttering a powerful spell that translates as "Paralyze His Senses!" and I knew no more.

When I awoke, I was still in Shetvan's wagon. But I was chained to it, insane with a bottomless bloodlust. I was lying down, and Shetvan stood menacingly over me. I triumphantly noticed the ugly wound on Shetvan's muzzle where I had clawed him.

"You! You are my problem!" he bellowed.

Absentmindedly, I noticed my left foreleg was mangled at the joint between my foot and my leg. I roared back and jumped up on three feet, looking him in the eye.

"I am your problem? You are a dirty, underhanded murderer, thief, and a liar, yet you call me your problem?!?" I demanded.

Shetvan laughed harshly. "I have to agree with you there! But you are a prudent young wolf who challenges his elders as he would those of his own rank!"

My eyes shone with hatred. "If I may remind you, I am *above* your rank!" I viciously pointed out.

Shetvan had no response for this. Then, to Shetvan and Draz's amazement, I snapped the chains that held my paws, ignoring the excruciating pain coming from the broken wrist. Quickly, I found Hacea.

Aran? Is that you?

Yes. Listen, I need you to get Shadow and Demon out here. Point them toward Guilyed.

Guilyed?!? He said he was taking you to a minor outpost!

I'll explain later.

Done!

Thanks, Hacea. Stay safe!

And you.

We broke contact. I let out a paranormal howl that shook the earth. The team of ten horses that pulled the caravan reared and whinnied.

I was salivating; it slathered from my lips, flecked with foam. My eyes were bloodshot, my bared fangs glinted in the setting sun. "You! You will die!" I roared in a sharp, bold voice. I planted my right forepaw so the floorboards shook. "You and I, Shetvan, will fight. Alone. Without that despicable werewolf you call an advisor!"

Enraged, Draz sprang at me, but I was ready. I slashed at his throat. Draz staggered back. I heard guards coming. Fifteen at least. I took my chance and attacked Shetvan. But this time, he was ready. He slugged me in the chest. I returned the blow. He, too, staggered away, grimacing and howling with pain.

Suddenly, I felt arrows sprouting from my thigh. I whipped around. Eighteen guards stood at the door, crossbows aimed at me. I reared and lunged. A minute later, five of them fell, never to rise again, and four hastily retreated. The remaining nine were wounded and shaky. I sported merely a bitten ear, slashed muzzle, and a bruised hind right leg. Most unfortunately, I did not hear Draz creeping up behind me. He hissed, *"Shzlan!"* and I collapsed.

CHAPTER THIRTEEN

Death Sentence

I was stiff when I awoke and could hardly move. The chains on my legs were relatively short, so I was confined to pacing in a tight circle. I quickly healed my wounds. I opened my mind, but nothing familiar reached me. I was in Guilyed.

I was in a small, earth-bare cell with a rough, woolen rug. I assumed it was around midday, because the small, barred window in my cell showed almost no shadow.

Outside the solid iron door, I could hear the clacking claws of a ten-wolf squad. Using my special abilities, I sensed they were armed with crossbows and longbows; swords; daggers; a few hidden knives; and a quiver of twelve arrows, each fletched with Griffin feathers. Talk about being armed! They were obviously expecting me to attempt an escape. Not likely. I noticed a small slot in the bottom of the iron door. *I wonder what it's for?* I thought, curling into a ball and waiting.

After what seemed like hours later, the slot opened, and a metal tray slid in. On it was a shallow basin of water and a platter with chunks of meat piled on it. I neutralized the drug and dug in. Minutes later, the tray was empty. I needed to do something, which is difficult when confined to pacing in a tight circle. Practicing the Old Tongue wasn't an option; if somebody came barging in here, my secret would be out. Singing "The Song of the Spirits?" Worth a shot to see if there was any advice.

At the fourth lyric, I was cut short. "Hey, Wolfie Boy! Can it! No trying out for the opera!" yelled a gruff, ridiculing voice.

I managed to hold my tongue long enough to come up with an answer. "Of course, sir. I'd forgotten my manners!" I retorted through gritted teeth. The other guards snickered loudly.

"Laugh now, Bait Breath! You won't be for long!" growled the timber wolf, throwing his companions a vehement look. He was a sergeant named Klaukos.

"Sure, Klaukos! Sure! Just get me all riled up and let Shetvan deal with you later. That's the way to do it!" I taunted.

Klaukos turned to stone. "How did…you …my name!?!" he stammered. I remained silent. "Bait Breath! How?" Klaukos demanded. "Wolfie Boy, do I have to come in… ." Klaukos stopped short and gulped.

"KLAUKOS!" Draz shouted furiously. "YOU ARE NOT TO SPEAK TO THE PRISONER!"

"I'm sorry, your grace. I...I couldn't control my tongue," Klaukos apologized.

"This is your tongue's last chance, Klaukos. If it happens again...," Draz, through clenched teeth, ended on a threatening note. "Guards! Take Aran to the Pit."

I took up a fighting stance as the door opened, and seven of the guards sprang in. I gave them a fight, but my efforts were futile. We exited the cell, eight bloody, one chained. We walked about a quarter of a mile before a large marble door opened, and we walked through.

Present in the cavernous chamber beyond the gate were three companies, dukes, duchesses, lords, ladies, and, of course, Shetvan. I must admit, he was dressed splendidly. Gold shirt, pants, circlet, and silver cape. His insignia was a black devil wolf with red eyes, bullhorns and wings in colored thread battling a unicorn with pure white skin, silver hooves, gold mane, tail, beard, and horn with an emerald eye. It was vivid and entrancing. *Show off!*

It was an odd time to think about it, but Shetvan was Shadow's age, not much older than me. And Hacea was the same age as I am. I wondered...nah! Suddenly, I was snapped from my thoughts by some high-pitched, bell-like voices.

No! I thought desperately. *It can't be them!*

But I was wrong, and it was too late. Lily, Rose, and Bibbles were in the tight grip of a few guards near the edge of the chasm of which even *I* couldn't see. I kept my cool, and Shetvan stepped regally onto the platform in the middle of the chamber.

"Dukes, duchesses, lords, and ladies, we come together to judge the strength of a rebel. Aran by name," Shetvan said. At this a gasp arose from the crowds.

One duke shouted out, "The legendary spirit? He will punish you foolish ones!"

And another, "Shetvan, you bring doom upon us all!"

"Silence! He is harmless!" Shetvan insisted.

"Really, Shetvan? Explain, then, your marred muzzle and bound chest!" I challenged with a snarl and murderous glare.

A chorus of, "Yes, indeed!" and "Truly, how so?" arose from the parliament.

"Well, I was...unprepared! Aran took advantage of me!" Shetvan protested.

"That's not what I heard Draz saying!" exclaimed one.

"You lie!" said another.

The room broke into an unending sea of voices.

"SILENCE!" roared Shetvan, angrier than a Devil Wolf. "Listen to me!"

He glared at the crowd in a cold, calm way, the way his voice sounded. Quickly, the crowd quieted. Draz entered the room and stood beside Shetvan. He wore a grey shirt, pants, silver circlet, and black cape. The werewolf's sigil was a devil wolf on one side and a human shaman on the other. It was done in gold, crimson, and black thread.

"Aran, you know we will let your friends go at the price of your surrender!" Draz jeered. I willed him to not go on. "Or you can be free, but the fairies <u>die</u>!" Draz swept his paw toward my three companions and the Pit. "Well! Which shall it be?" Draz demanded. I swallowed hard.

Hacea, I hope you can understand my decision. I opened my mouth to speak.

"No, Wilder! We won't let you surrender!" cried Rose bravely. Lily nodded as Rose took her hand. Clutching Bibbles between them, they threw themselves into the Pit with a brave war cry.

"NO!" I yelled, snapping my chains and lunging for the Pit. I skidded to a stop at the edge, and a white, chalky spray of dust and pebbles flew up. But I was too late. My mind, freshly healed, snapped twice as hard. Time stood still, and the phrase "Thy most faithful friends shall be thy greatest weakness" flashed across my mind. As time sped up again, I wheeled toward Shetvan, my heart intent on murder.

Draz snarled, "Guards! Attack!"

I ducked beneath the path of a deadly arrow before my true spirit took over, and I perceived but simple thoughts as the room descended into pandemonium. Slash. Duck. Twist. Bite. Defend! Attack! Shetvan's brutal laughter ringing out. A slash of crimson steel. Nothingness as my mind faded away.

It may have been a dream, but I thought I heard Klaukos laughing cruelly, "Lock 'im up, boys. He ain't coming out for a long, long time."

CHAPTER FOURTEEN

Reckonings

When I awoke, my mind whirled. *I lunge for the chasm. Rose and Lily disappear into the blackness. No!* Shakily, I sat up and focused. I was back in my cell. And along with my now-too-familiar throbbing head, I thought, *What if Hacea is Shetvan's future spouse?*

The thought drained me, and I collapsed on the rug. I realized it was night as faint moonbeams flickered along my fur. For the first time in a long time, I was unchained. I looked up at the moon and howled. I cried for what I had lost, what I had to lose, and then lost consciousness as a strange sense of safety lulled me to sleep.

For a week, I stayed that way. I ate only enough to survive and moved only to bay at the moon. And I thought about Hacea every possible second. Then, the night that the moon was nearly full, I heard a nearly imperceptible sound of wing beats. They were soft and quick. Then, an ash-grey owl with kind, blue eyes flew into my cell. It was

Luvlissa, spirit of kindness and consolation. She had a soft, soothing voice.

"Greetings, Aran. You are faring ill," Luvlissa nodded thoughtfully.

I smiled, and my lips cracked as I croaked, "Yes, I am. I'm glad you could come."

"You are sad and wasting away. Be cautious, Aran. Many lives are dependent on yours. Ah, yes. I came here from Wildspirit Castle. They are in danger! Due to misinformation, Kalabar will attack with Hacea still there. You must escape." Luvlissa explained urgently. "I must go now. Take care!" She flew out the window.

And Wilder, a familiar voice entered my mind, *in thy greatest sorrow, remember who you are!*

Hacea? Is that you? I thought joyously.

Yes, it's me. Don't get hurt, all right? We need you.

I won't.

Stay safe!

We broke contact.

I've got to get out of here! I thought. *Gruffin?*

Aran?

Yes! Tell Shadow and Demon to enter at the East Gate and to blend in!

Consider it done. Good luck!

Thanks!

That was out of my way. Now, how did I get out? Again, the idea came back to me. Suddenly, I had a plan.

Hacea, just so you know.

I told her everything, including my plan.

I can do my part, if you do yours! Hacea concluded.

Then, pack your bags tonight and be ready to move to Guilyed! And please grab The Orb. It's under my bed.

I will, Hacea promised.

I smiled. The next part of the plan: listen to the guards.

"Well, apart from me winning the tournament, the only thing that is new, far as I can tell, is that Shetvan's wedding Lady Hacea next month. And he is one lucky son of a gun to be getting that diamond!" chuckled a young timber wolf named Sergeant Foxeye.

"I heard he was doing it next week!" scoffed Klaukos. "Although I do agree with you on the last part!"

Foxeye began to say something else when a resounding, "ATTENTION!" echoed through the corridor.

Draz, what perfect timing! I smirked.

When Draz was just outside my door, I sighed in the most longing, wistful voice I could muster, "If Shetvan weds Hacea, I don't know what I'll do!"

Draz paused. Then, he entered my cell.

"Well, well, well. How are you today, Aran?" purred Draz, who seemed *very* happy.

"Draz. The sniveling, groveling, obedient pet of Shetvan. What a pleasure!" The first word was a challenge, but the rest was pure sarcasm. The others were surprised to see me so refreshed and like myself.

"I see you're the same as ever," Draz remarked disdainfully.

"What do you want?" I yawned, bored.

"To tell you that Shetvan has something to tell you."

"You speak in riddles, as well as play with them? How boring," I drawled, scratching an itch.

Draz ignored my comment. "This will be a bit more formal. You will wear this," Draz said and handed me a bundle. He turned and exited the cell.

The bundle contained a white cotton shirt; a heavy, stiff leather vest and belt; black leggings; and a golden pendant with a ruby in the shape of a compass. I pulled them on and growled, "Open up!"

The guards watched me with distrustful eyes, and Klaukos sneered at my shaggy coat, cold eyes, and calm appearance. I snorted arrogantly.

"You wanna go, Klaukos? 'Cause I can guarantee I'll come out on top."

Klaukos didn't respond, but he kept his paw on his sword.

Foxeye trotted down the corridor, and I followed, with Klaukos at my heels. I had it all figured out: Shetvan would try to be nice to me, but then use me as a bargaining chip to convince Hacea to come to Guilyed. We arrived at a walnut oak door, gilded with gems, gold, copper, and bronze. A wolf stood on either side of the door. Klaukos knocked lightly. The door opened, and a deep, powerful voice said, "Master Aran, you may enter."

I stepped in, and the door slid shut. I was amazed to see a tan, black haired, well-dressed dwarf. He was rather tall…for a dwarf.

"Greetings, Master Aran. I am Turin of Nienor, from Nargthrand. Come this way, if you please."

Turin led me to a curtained doorway, where he stepped aside. I entered the room and dipped my head curtly.

"You sent for me, Shetvan?" I asked in a slightly hostile tone.

"Yes, I did. There are things we must discuss," Shetvan replied, leaning against the wall of the parlor with his paws in his pockets. He pushed off the wall and walked into a different room. I followed him in. Well, someone was irritable today. "Ceris, bring in the meal!" he called in a loud but kind tone.

In stepped another dwarf, a woman with long flaxen hair wearing a deep green dress and a white apron.

"This is Turin's wife. They have served me faithfully for many years," Shetvan introduced me.

"Yes, my husband and I have been treated very well by Master Shetvan," Ceris said in an airy, musical tone.

The noon meal consisted of reindeer steaks and hare stew. For dessert, there were salty antlers with some meat hanging off in delicious, chewable tatters and hooves glazed in ptarmigan broth.

"We will eat, then talk," Shetvan said.

We dug in with gusto, but in a mannerly fashion-a most complex maneuver. Licking our lips, we returned to the parlor, sitting in two black, gold, and red armchairs.

"Now, you may already know about this because of...What's his name? Klawos, Skulkos...?"

"Klaukos, Shetvan. Klaukos."

"Klaukos; ah, yes! Because of Klaukos's big mouth. I intend to wed Hacea."

"Yes, sometime next week?" I inquired in false ignorance.

"No, tomorrow," Shetvan corrected.

I imitated being stricken with grief. I barely managed to continue in a straight voice...because I was laughing so hard inside.

"I see. So you brought me here to gloat," I said.

Shetvan was acting perfectly according to my plan!

"If it is not unwelcome," *It is,* "I wish to invite you to the wedding." Shetvan ignored me and continued, saying, "I also wish to ask you to stay in one of the guest chambers so you may accompany me tomorrow morning."

You should have seen his eyes, the way he said it! Somehow, I was sure there was something he was hiding.

I resolved to think about it later. "I accept because I have no choice. What will we do now, then?"

Shetvan smiled. "If you would like, we could play Stone Alpha." Stone Alpha! It was my favorite game.

"You're on!" I grinned deviously. Shetvan was going to be disappointed!

❧

Hacea waited anxiously at Wildspirit for Shetvan's letter. She had sent Apache with clothing, money, and more provisions for Shadow and Demon. She had even relocated The Orb beneath her bed. But she could not wait. She stamped her paw in anger and impatience. *Where is it?* she thought.

"Lady Hacea?" called a familiar voice.

"Forrest, is that you?" asked Hacea, opening the door. In stepped a rough-furred chestnut wolf with streaks of white fur along his front legs and face. He limped slightly on his left foreleg.

"Message from Lord Shetvan, milady. Looks like an invitation of sorts," Forrest replied.

"Thank you, Forrest. You know what to do. Two days leave. Hunting upon return," Hacea said.

Forrest bowed deeply and left. Hacea ripped open the envelope. The letter said:

My Dearest Hacea,

I have waited for an opportunity, and now have the chance, to ask your paw in marriage. The celebration is the afternoon of the morrow, so please come quickly. All will be ready upon your arrival. Your friend, Aran, will be attending. And I have a surprise involving him! I wish you a safe journey, dearest.

Your Love,

Shetvan

Hacea rolled her eyes as she read the first three sentences (as if she couldn't refuse!) but became concerned as she read the fourth and fifth. *Shetvan's using him as a bargaining chip, as we expected, but what's this about the surprise?* She cleared her mind and, straightening her attire, walked swiftly to The Council. They had much to discuss.

CHAPTER FIFTEEN

Free Again

After playing eleven epic games of Stone Alpha, I won nine and lost two. Shetvan was in an ornery mood. He had no reason to be; I was a skillful player.

For the evening meal, there was ptarmigan potpie and pheasant a la king with a side of two plump rabbits and elderberry wine. For dessert, there was a beautiful berry pie, liberally sprinkled with a combination of sugar and berry juice, which formed a pleasant syrup. It was delicious!

As the purple light outside turned to coal black, Turin, Ceris, Shetvan, and I sat around a roaring fire in the parlor on rich, soft cushions and played a game of Riddles. There were some tricky ones, too! We played rather late, but when the stars shone like snowy jewels in the black velvet sky, we finally retired. The dwarves bid us good evening, and Shetvan and I left for our separate quarters.

Shetvan's rooms were a different style than Hacea's. His was a bright green pine theme, with the pines on the walls painted in realistic patterns and colors; fox skins on the floor; and tan bedrock in the corner containing the pool. The bed was a darker pine green. The curtains were patterned after the walls but in the bed's dark green color. On the canopy, you could see the tips of the trees; the dark, dark sky; and the full moon in the middle.

My room was similar to Demon's at Wildspirit. It was an icy silver room, walls painted with towering birches, floor carpeted with polar bear skins, the bed whitish-silver, and the pool on a black sheet of bedrock. The curtains were reflections of the walls, and the canopy showed the tips of the ghostly birches, the crisp indigo sky, and a burning rust moon. I eyed my new prison and sighed. Then, I curled up on the bed and fell asleep.

I woke early in the morning and froze. The door to my room was opening!

Someone's going to kill me! I thought.

I crept out of my bed on the side farthest from the door and around to the side, where I crouched tensely, waiting. The trespasser walked up to the edge of the bed, and I pounced.

"AHHHHH!" cried a familiar voice.

I backed down instantly. "Turin, is that you? I'm <u>so</u> sorry! I thought you were an assassin!" I gulped, turning red with embarrassment.

"No harm done," Turin said, cheerful as ever. I raised my eyebrow skeptically, because he was limping. "Well, maybe a little," he said, grimacing. I had broken his ankle.

"Here, one minute, just hold still! *Heilzren!*" I said quickly.

Turin looked at me, astounded, gasping like a fish out of water.

"Not a word!" I demanded.

Turin shook his head. Then, we went to breakfast.

Ceris had laid a fine spread: oatmeal with cubes of rich meat; a light beaver broth with dumplings; and a bowl of tart, refreshing fruit. Soon after that, Turin put on his hat, and we left for the tailor's shop. Apparently, Shetvan wanted me in finer apparel for the wedding.

When we arrived at the shop, the tailor had already laid out many clothes.

"Good day to you, Master Turin, Master Aran. I have selected my finest for you!" he gestured in a thick, rich accent.

I chose quickly: a ruffled white shirt, a grey leather vest with my seal in black and cobalt thread, black leather pants, and a silver pendant with a star sapphire adorning it.

Turin selected a copper shirt, scarlet pants, and a half-cape over his right shoulder. His shirt was embroidered in scarlet thread with a strange symbol, which I later learned was a Dwarven symbol meaning 'War Hawk'. His pendant was a large ruby ornamented in gold. We paid for our purchases and headed back to Shetvan's quarters.

As we waded through the busy streets, I glimpsed Shadow and Demon buying food. They didn't see me, and I looked away before Turin's sharp eyes could follow mine. Turin and I returned to Shetvan's parlor.

We dressed and checked our attire. Turin looked superb, my fur was smooth as silk, and Ceris's silver-blue gown was elegant with her pearl pendant. Shetvan's golden suit with white pants went handsomely with his Celtic knot of gold. We waited in the courtyard for an ivory carriage pulled by a black Appaloosa stallion and an almost identical mare. Shetvan firmly escorted me by the arm into the carriage. Soon we were on our way.

Hacea moaned inside. She tried on the eleventh dress and decided she liked it – for her own sake, lest she be there all day. The serving wolves liked it, too. It was a silvery-white gown with copper embroideries that brought out the color in her eyes. Her delicate silver and topaz copper amulet matched the silvery tiara.

She waited in a side room where Shetvan told her he'd meet her. She watched Aran, Turin, Ceris, Shadow, and Demon file inside, and she noticed the two dragons submersing themselves in the lake beside the chapel. The pews quickly filled up, and then Shetvan walked to her side.

"Milady," he knelt and kissed Hacea's paw. Shetvan rose and smiled charmingly. He looked very pleased with himself.

Here comes his mystery surprise, Hacea thought.

"As you know, since Aran is my prisoner, I may do with him as I wish. So," Shetvan opened his arms, "I am giving Aran to you as your personal servant!"

Hacea pretended to be thrilled with Shetvan's gift.

"Why, thank you! I can't think of a way to repay you!" Hacea gushed, using her most alluring voice to lower Shetvan's defenses.

"Well, if you don't tell, I won't," Shetvan winked, then pulled her close and gave her a quick peck on the cheek before releasing her.

Hacea struggled to keep herself from slapping Shetvan across the face.

Wilder, if you're listening, I'm going to get you for that!

I was, and I gulped at the thought of what she was going to do to me. *So that's why he was trying to be nice to me,* I mused as they began the vows. *Showtime,* I thought. I felt the minds of the assembly and picked out one, a young, tan-furred female. I whispered *"Shzlan!"* and she crumpled.

Seven people shrieked at once, and Shetvan ran to see what was wrong. In the pandemonium that ensued, Shadow, Demon, Hacea, and I slipped out the door. The two dragons shedded the lake water, and Hacea and I rode Apache, while my brothers rode Gruffin. We sped toward Kalabar's camp.

"So," I asked cautiously, "just how do you intend to get me back for that little incident with Shetvan?"

"Like this," Hacea said.

Then, she lunged for me. When she came up for air, I blinked like an owl and didn't say anything. Hacea hummed and stared at the black Appaloosas that were running beneath us, as if nothing had happened. The other four snickered loudly.

"Oh, shut up!" I growled.

Sometimes, I don't understand why Hacea does things. Mind you, I do appreciate them.

CHAPTER SIXTEEN

Kalabar

Soon the dragons reached the walls bordering the hunting grounds, and we landed.

"Apache, Gruffin, go find Kalabar's camp. Take Shadow and Demon with you," I said.

The two dragons nodded and took off. Hacea and I waited to confront the horses. They cantered into the clearing seconds later. The stallion snorted and neighed at us. Then, he reared and charged at Hacea. I pulled her out of his path as he hurtled past.

A flash of recognition lit Hacea's eyes. "Shyma, it's me!" she barked.

The Appaloosa stopped short at his mare's side. Then, to my amazement, the air around them began to shimmer with a soft, warm, golden light. They grew feathering on their legs and a single horn of black light rose from their brows. They were unicorns!

"My apologies, Hacea. I had forgotten you. It has been a year!" the stallion whickered playfully.

Hacea smiled.

"Hacea, do you remember me? I'm Darma," said the mare. Hacea nodded to her question. "Shyma and I were kidnapped by Draz last summer, but something went wrong, and we managed to escape. We stayed in our horse form until we were recaptured as working horses."

To me, Hacea said, "This is Shyma. He's Kalabar's son, and Darma is his fiancée." Then, she turned back to the unicorns. "How did you escape?" Hacea inquired anxiously.

"Right before your service, two strange wolves came and unbuckled our harnesses and released us," Shyma explained.

His description matched that of my brothers.

"Gruffin must have recognized them as I did and told Aran's brothers to free you," Hacea mused.

The two unicorns froze.

"This is *Aran*?" exclaimed Darma. Hacea nodded, and the two unicorns knelt.

"That's it! I'm hitting myself on the head the next time someone does that!" I threatened. It was so weird, all these famous people bowing to me just because I was suddenly Aran.

Shyma's eyes were wide, and he shook his head. "It's an honor, Lord Aran. It's just that it was…unexpected."

As he said this, a faint buzzing noise filled my head. I shook my head, but to no avail.

Aran. Aran! <u>ARAN!</u>

Apache? Is that you?

Yes, stone ears. I found the camp. Come quickly.

Thanks, Apache.

"What was that about?" Hacea asked. I told her what had happened.

Shyma and I found the landmarks Apache had given us, Darma and Hacea trailing us. Soon, we saw the unicorns' standard: the silver horn, tipped with blood, plunged through a black heart laced with chains. Bugles announced our arrival.

Shyma reared and trumpeted gaily. He and Darma bolted through the maze of tents. Hacea and I exchanged glances and rushed headlong after them. As we beheld Kalabar's headquarters, I whistled in surprise. This was not a tent as I had imagined.

"He's been here for a while, hasn't he?" I teased Hacea. She elbowed me in the gut. Hard. I doubled over in pain. "I thought so!" I whispered hoarsely, my eyes watering.

Sturdy stone walls, tiled roof, a tower, double guards, the works. It was like a miniature castle! From the tower flew the standard.

Then, there was the unicorn's leader himself. He was a dappled blue roan with black legs, hooves, mane, muzzle, beard, and tail. His eyes were a piercing blue, and his horn was a twist of black and white light, tapering to a threatening point. His left eye had a scar over it, a jagged line, the work of a wolf's sword. It reminded me of Storm's scar.

"Kalabar, I have dreamed of the day we might unite openly," Hacea decreed, kneeling. I followed her example.

"Why is it that The Night Warrior and The Dawn Fighter kneel before me, an old war pony?" boomed Kalabar in a broad, rich laugh. "It is I," Kalabar stated, "who should kneel to you!"

His words matched his actions, and the other unicorns (who, along with my companions, had gathered during the brief exchange) knelt as well.

Slowly, I rose, and Hacea followed suit. Just as slowly, one clap turned into a sea of applause.

"Thank you, all of you!" I shouted earnestly. "But I couldn't have done it without my friends." I gestured at those in the crowd and put my paw around Hacea's shoulder, who had stepped closer. "And I wouldn't be here right now," I said quietly as the applause dwindled away, "if two fairies and a Burple had not given their lives for me and saved my life three times on this journey."

The crowd was silent. I looked to the Spirit Mountains, hoping my friends were there.

"Oh, Wilder!" Hacea whispered tenderly, resting her head on my shoulder.

Shadow and Demon bowed their heads, biting their lips. Cautiously, Kalabar stoked up our moods.

"We will avenge these deaths! We will defeat Shetvan!" he trumpeted. A cheer started up. "But if we are to emerge victorious, we must be ready! Prepare yourselves for the coming ordeal!" Kalabar bugled, whipping the crowd into a frenzy. Battle cries rang in my ears.

I smiled and, looking at my friends, began to chant The Song of the Spirits. My friends and I sang the first two verses, but everyone joined in the last three. We sang it once more, and then the crowd dispersed into the tents, readying for battle. Shyma trotted over.

"Aran," he began.

"Pardon me, but please call me Wilder. Just until the battle," I said. Shyma nodded.

"Wilder, my father wishes to speak to you and your companions. And about the others... ," Shyma paused, distressed he would say the wrong thing.

I smiled painfully. "There's nothing you could've done, Shyma. Wait one moment," I said as I beckoned to my companions, who quickly caught up. We followed Shyma, and on the way, I asked him a few questions. "So Shyma, where's your mother?"

"Dead."

"I'm sorry. How?"

"A warrior. But he is gone. We made sure of that," Shyma said. He was thinking of his father. "She was a beautiful golden appaloosa with a white mane and tail and an Indian blaze. Her name was Honeysuckle." Shyma's voice was filled with longing, and a plan formed in my head.

We arrived at the fortress, and Darma opened the doors. She led us to a large chamber, which held a map of Arkamish with representational markers on it. As we took our seats, Kalabar entered, wearing a black vest and a cape fastened with a garnet brooch.

"I've called you into council to discuss your strategies. You see," Kalabar explained in response to our puzzled faces, "you will be partnered up to command a battalion of the army." This was met by many gasps and shocked looks.

"Shyma and Darma, Shadow and Demon, and Apache and Gruffin, you will be in charge with a trusted general nearby. Wilder, you and Hacea will be at my side." I nodded. "Now, we need to discuss the placement of Shetvan's troops," Kalabar self-consciously glanced at Hacea, revealing our source.

Kalabar pointed to the markers for emphasis. "There is a hoard of minotaurs outside of Siruka, a throng of ogres near Kálariátal, and a combination of basilisks and manticores near Flisma. The rest of the troops are marching here from Guilyed. Storm will lead the Minotaurs; Red is leading the ogres; Klaukos is leading the basilisks and manticores; and Shetvan, Draz, and Thunder-Eye will lead the main force.

"Shyma and Darma, you will take a herd of unicorns to Flisma. Shadow, Demon, you will take three packs of wolves to Siruka. Apache and Gruffin, you will take a horde of dragons and hydras to Kálariátal. Then, Aran, Hacea, and I will take the main force to Guilyed," Kalabar concluded, drinking a glass of water offered by one of the guards.

Darma spoke, "Those of you without armor follow me." Shadow, Demon, and Apache started to file out of the room.

"Aran, you and Hacea please stay here," Kalabar said. Shyma took the hint and left. We turned and walked back to the table. The great oak doors boomed shut, leaving us alone with the unicorn leader. "Tonight is the Moon of the Wolf. According to legend, it is the night of the final transformation," Kalabar said gravely, "for you both."

"This isn't a joke, is it?" I asked with black humor.

Wordlessly, he shook his head.

"I want you to come tonight when it is done. We'll fit you for equipment then," Kalabar instructed.

Nodding, Hacea and I left the room. I followed a guard who led me to my black tent and then led Hacea to hers. My tent held a cot, a mirror, and a stand with a basin of fresh water. I felt the Orb of the Eagle's Eye beneath the bed. Hacea had kept her promise. I removed my attire and slowly drifted off to sleep. I dreamed of my parents. Each in turn warned me with one of Hacea's verses, 'As the moon gains fullness, so does his strength'. The full moon rose.

CHAPTER SEVENTEEN

Spirit Form

The moon illuminated the tent when I awoke to an acute pain in my shoulder blades.

"Ahhhhhhggg!" I groaned. I sprang off the cot, shaking myself awake. I splashed cold water on my face and crouched in front of the mirror.

Slowly, my silver wings sprung from my back, tipped with black talons. My mouth was numb, and my serrated teeth curved lethally. Icy sparks smarted in my nose. A black leather vest materialized, my seal embroidered in cyan, black, and silver. My claws became silver lightning, and my silver coat turned to semi-lucid shadow.

Every smell came in sharp and clear as my senses became enhanced. My eyes were sharp, but it was hard to tell anything else about them, because they pierced through the mirror when I tried to look at them. Every word in my vocabulary was partnered with one in the Old Tongue.

Abruptly, a chilling, agonizing frost raced through my veins. I let out a clear, spectral howl, which chilled the air around me. Seconds later, Hacea howled in a similar way, and I raced out of the tent. I had to find Hacea!

I ran to Hacea's forest-green tent, feeling Demon and Shadow hurrying toward her tent as well. I burst into the tent, and the excruciating cold left me.

"Are you all right?" I exclaimed.

"Yes…I'm fine." she groaned.

Demon and Shadow bolted into the tent, skidding to a halt. "Are they okay? We heard their calls!" Demon huffed, eyes flying around the room.

"Where are Aran and Hacea?" demanded Shadow.

"Yeah, where are they?" Demon roared.

Great, they've never seen us in spirit form! I thought, exasperated.

"Hey, DUMBON! We're standing right in front of you!" I said. Demon looked skeptical, making my blood boil. "Don't make me come over there, Demon!" I seethed.

"Wilder? Is that you in the silver wings and fur?" Shadow asked sheepishly. I nodded, cooling off. "Well, it's kind of hard to tell. We've never seen you like this before!" Shadow protested in self-defense.

Glancing at Hacea's mirror, I whistled in surprise. My eyes were an icy silver-blue.

Then, I looked carefully at Hacea. "Wow!" I said. She was stunning! Her reddish fur had a black-gold shadow, her wings a griffin's with gold feathers. Her teeth were curved and could have cut a fine thread. Fiery sparks smarted in her nostrils. Her black leather vest, coat of arms embroidered in red, gold, and silver thread, was perfect. Her claws looked like golden lightning, and her eyes were a marvelous copper. Hacea blushed in embarrassment.

"We should go meet Kalabar now," Hacea intoned.

"We'll meet you later!" Demon called as Hacea and I took off, flying swiftly to Kalabar's fortress. We were immediately taken to Kalabar.

"Wow!" Kalabar whistled in surprise. He shook himself. "Come, then. We must hurry. We march at dawn, and it is the third hour now."

I nodded, and we filed out of the citadel. To our amazement, two satiny black wings sprouted from Kalabar's withers! Hacea and I gasped.

"You're...you're a Unicus!" I sputtered in pure astonishment.

Kalabar and Hacea stared at me, bewildered.

"How did you know that?" Kalabar demanded with a steely glare.

"My…my father taught me," I explained, unsure of myself. Kalabar inhaled sharply. "What?" I asked uneasily.

"What was your father's name, Aran?" Kalabar queried harshly, eyes closed, teeth clenched.

"Shamar."

Kalabar flinched, as if he'd been struck. "So it was meant to be again."

Understanding washed over Hacea. Her eyes widened, and she bit her lip.

"What is it?" I asked queasily.

Kalabar grimaced, "Shamar…Shamar was Shetvan's father."

CHAPTER EIGHTEEN

Betrayals Before Battle

I was dazed and jolted by Kalabar's revelation. Then, my shock burned down to bitter fury. "Do you mean to say that <u>fiend</u> is my brother?" I demanded.

"Yes," Kalabar sighed.

"Then," I barked, "you also mean to say that hellhound murdered our parents?" My eyes grew cold with rage.

"Yes, Aran. Yes," Hacea whispered softly.

Cursing, I took off. Why me? Why hadn't they told me this before? What would happen if people found out? Or if Shadow and Demon did? Were they even my brothers? I blinked away the tears and howled my misery to the skies.

Kalabar regretted withholding the information from Aran for so long. It had truly shattered the boy. They watched in agony as he took off. Even now, as he howled, Aran was at the breaking point. Kalabar wondered if he'd ever recover. Glancing at Hacea in misery, he shook his head. "We'll have to wait for Aran to come to us," he said.

"It's just so much for him to have to understand at once. But at least we finally told him. The weight of it all...if we hadn't now, it would've broken his spirit," Hacea sighed bitterly.

Kalabar agreed, and they trudged back to the castle.

Eventually, my anger simmered down, and I felt calm enough to fly back. That's when I saw a familiar snake. Surdel. But what really grabbed my interest was the fact that Sizcèl, one of our spies, was hurriedly speaking to him, pointing at a map. *That defective, conspiring traitor!* I thought. I dove with the speed of a falcon and murmured, "*Èinshlafrn!*"

The two spies fell limply to the ground. With ease, I slung them over my back and flew toward Kalabar's fortress.

Hacea, tell Kalabar's guards I'm coming. Can't stop now. Be there soon!

All right. And Aran, she stopped me before I broke away, *I'm so sorry.*

I closed my eyes, hardening my thoughts.

It doesn't matter. I'm not my brother! I flew swifter and walled my mind, not giving Hacea the chance to respond. But I could sense her pain. *Lords*, I thought bitterly, *why am I so sensitive around her?*

I glided into the entrance and trotted into the map room. Kalabar, Shyma, Darma, Hacea, and the guards were waiting expectantly. Hacea, although hiding it very well, was hurting. I allowed some of my regret, pain, and sorrow to flow past my mental wall to Hacea, hoping she would understand.

She rewarded my efforts with a sad smile of under-standing, as well as an unexpected gentleness. *What's she trying to tell me?* I wondered. I walked forward and low-ered my shoulder, allowing the two snakes to fall to the cold marble floor. My four friends' eyes were sparkling and filled with questions. "Sizcèl was leaking informa-tion to Surdel," I said.

"Why that rotten, cursed, treacherous, treasonous scum!" Kalabar swore vehemently. Darma whispered something in Shyma's ear. He chuckled quietly. Kalabar, on a knife's edge, snapped, "Shyma! What are you laugh-ing at?"

Composing himself, Shyma responded, "Father, I must apologize, but Darma pointed out it was ironic that the penalty for treason is being burned at the stake, and the offender's name is Sizcèl."

Kalabar must have paused for a millisecond before snorting.

"I am glad to see that my son and daughter-in-law-to-be have a sense of humor in these dark times," Kalabar said, clearing his throat. "Now, we must proceed. Askrie," Kalabar motioned toward a dapple-grey guard, "take these two to the dungeons. Give them a good quantity of the Schwarz Diÿe Schlägurs Dürre to keep them out for the battle."

"Yes, Kalabar," Askrie replied, collecting the offenders and trotting away under the stormy, slate sky.

That'll be one heck of a storm for the battle, I thought.

"You two!" Kalabar neighed. "Follow me to the smithy. We must collect your armor." He turned and trotted away.

Upon reaching the forge, we were given two options for armor: The first was made from black and silver shed dragon skin, gilded with jewels. The second was a lighter armor of a deep grey. It was made of dragon scales, splintered dragon knucklebones, and phoenix feathers smelted together, with the result blessed by a unicorn's horn. It was woven with spells that caused the wearer to blend in with their surroundings. Hacea and I chose the second variety, which had been Kalabar's choice as well.

The smiths, who were the finest in the land, forged our armor with a great deal of magic. Then, it was time for the vital weapon to be created.

My sword had a hilt of obsidian reinforced with platinum, a single bright lapis lazuli set in silver embedded in the center. The blade's core was of soft silver to prevent the blade from snapping. The outer layer was a steel of dragon talons and obsidian platinum. It was two-and-a-quarter feet long, and I dubbed it Shadeslayer.

Hacea's sword had a hilt of gold and amber with three rubies set in copper on the pommel. The blade's core was of Wolfsrang, so it would give a little when necessary; the rest was dragon talons and hardened black gold reinforcement. It was two feet long, and she dubbed it Sunchaser.

When we practiced, it felt as though we had had swords with us forever, and we fought with great skill. Even Kalabar was shocked.

"This is amazing! How could you possibly have learned so well so quickly?" he exclaimed.

With a cold, harsh gleam in my eye, I whispered, "Then our enemies will be surprised as well."

Kalabar gazed upon me with new eyes, with a bit more respect and awe than before.

"You have grown, Aran. Both in wisdom and in personality," he nodded gravely.

"Am I not who I once was?" I acknowledged with a questioning lilt.

Kalabar and I stared down, each daring the other to make the next move. Hacea broke us up before we were at each other's throats.

"I think Aran and I have practiced long enough. We should contact the other commanders," she said.

I backed down; the coming onslaught had rubbed my nerves raw. We left for the fortress. Upon entering the map room, we were greeted by the new commanders: Shadow, Demon, Shyma, Darma, Apache, and Gruffin.

There were also some unicorn generals in their battle armor. Diego was a blood-bay stallion with a black face, horn, mane, and tail, with one green eye and one yellow eye. Tañgor was a golden-peach mare with one white sock, mane, tail, blaze, and horn. Her eyes were a grey-green. Dreamfighter was a white mare with fiery orange hooves, mane, tail, and horn. She had strong, bright turquoise eyes.

"Right, then. You all know where you are going, correct?" Kalabar asked. Affirmative murmurs filled the room. No one remarked on Kalabar's wings, but many surprised looks were shared. "Good," said Kalabar, "then go and gather your troops. Meet us at the entrance."

The room emptied quickly. Hacea and I followed Kalabar out of the hall.

The main force consisted of many wolves, unicorns, phoenixes, griffins, pegasi, dendroids (tree warriors), dragons, and a few others. One golden dragon named Cherokee was Apache's cousin. When we arrived at the entrance with the troops in tow, Kalabar, Hacea, and I proceeded to the top of the stairs in front of the entire camp. There Kalabar began.

"Warriors and peoples of Arkamish!" he trumpeted to the sea of cheers. "We have crawled too long in this shell of our home, turned wasteland by the demon! No longer will we live like vermin! Instead, we shall return Arkamish's former glory and rid this land of that menace!" Kalabar challenged. The crowd was screaming. "This day, in the twilight, we fight for revenge!"

"For revenge!" the crowd bellowed.

Energized, Kalabar went on. "FOR OUR LOVED ONES!"

"For our loved ones!" roared the frenzied mob.

"AND FOR FREEDOM!!!" Kalabar roared.

The crowd had been stoked to their capacity. They strained to be freed.

"THIS DAY, WE TAKE BACK WHAT IS OURS!" Kalabar yelled with a blood-lusting fierceness.

The troops broke to their stations, preparing to meet the adversary.

CHAPTER NINETEEN

Fight to the Finish

"Diego! You take the left-most flank! Tañgor! Right-most! Dreamfighter, your special operatives!" Kalabar ordered quickly. "Lady Hacea, Lord Aran. Take your places at the head of your army, if you please," Kalabar beckoned.

Smiling with grim determination, I watched as all the flyers unfurled their wings. Everyone, soldiers, healers, the unicorn leaders, Kalabar, and Hacea, was watching me expectantly. Taking a deep breath, I thought, *Right then. This is it.* I was ready.

With the weight of a thousand lives on my shoulders, I snarled, "CHAAARGE!!!" and pounded toward the road at full speed. A pack of war cries reached my ears, and I howled. That howl chilled to the bone, yet burned with energy. We burst onto the main road. I sniffed the air, peering into the murky darkness of twilight.

Hacea?

Yes?

Tell Kalabar I'm scouting ahead! I'll be back soon!

I took off, blending in perfectly with the night sky. Shetvan's train of warriors was about half a mile up the road. They had attempted to sneak up on us by taking a mountain passage. Now, they were stuck. If we attacked quickly, we would trap them against the canyon. Their only escape route was through a narrow ravine, where they would sustain heavy losses. I returned quickly to our troops.

"I have good news!" I exclaimed, gasping for breath. I told the generals everything I had seen. "But we must hurry, or we won't head them off at the pass!" I urged.

"You are an excellent scout, Lord Aran!" Dreamfighter said, clapping me on the back.

I nodded my thanks to her. The commanders informed the soldiers of the good news.

"Now, forward!" I roared.

We accelerated quickly once more. My muscles began to call for more speed, and I quickly outpaced the others. I felt the thrill of running down my prey, the ecstasy of tearing over the path, and the honor of earning my freedom. I was going faster, faster, faster as my wings hurled me forward. I raised a howl that was a challenge and a defiant rebellion. Closing my eyes with satisfaction, I slowed my pace and let the others catch up to me. We had reached the entrance to the canyon.

Hacea and I barked "Attack!!!" and drew our weapons. I leapt on an ogre and rent him from shoulder to hip, sword flashing, and began slicing my way through the ranks of Shetvan's forces.

The battle raged around me; blood and corpses were everywhere, and battle cries filled the air. I had just disposed of a Minotaur when I saw Hacea pinned down by a black dragon, Sunchaser buried in the brute's shoulder. I growled, gathered speed, and leapt. Extending Shadeslayer, I snarled, *"Feuyzr!"* Black flames flickered up the sides of my blade as the sword sank into the beast's heart. I rolled the fiend's corpse off of Hacea.

"Are you all right?" I asked Hacea.

"Yes, I'm fine," she groaned. As she stood, her left leg gave out. "Ahhhh! Maybe not so fine," she said through gritted teeth.

"Easy, easy. Hold on a minute," I assured her. *"Heilzren,"* I whispered.

Hacea shivered as her fur and muscles rippled, then stood.

"Thank you, Aran."

I retrieved her sword and handed it to her.

"No problem, Princess. See you when it's over!" I grinned fiercely before dancing away to fight once more. I clobbered a dwarf, then was thrown off my paws with a blow from an ogre's heavy club. Suddenly, Cherokee swooped out of the skies and beheaded the creature. "Thanks! I owe you one!" I whooped. Cherokee winked and took off once more. I followed him.

More black dragons filled the sky. One began to move toward Cherokee. It roared and swooped to attack. Then, my ice fire burned through it. The dragon was disintegrated into frosty particles, and Cherokee, who realized his good fortune, hollered, "I guess we're even!"

I grinned and began to attack the dragons, occasionally strafing the Minotaurs, manticores, and basilisks below with deadly frost.

A great wind had been blowing during the entire battle, and the pounding rain made it difficult for even me to see as the mud and blood mixed, and thunder and lightning lit up the dawn sky.

It seemed as though we were winning the battle when I spotted Shetvan. He was fighting side by side with Draz. They had just downed a phoenix, and Shetvan was sneering, "Take that, fool!"

My eyes blazed as I swooped downward.

Hacea, get over here! I just found Shetvan!

Be right there, Aran.

Soon, she arrived at my side as I deflected a blow from an enemy warrior. His sword missed its mark, my neck, but bit into my skin and scratched me from my right cheekbone to the corner of my mouth. She thrust Sunchaser through the wolf's ribs, and he collapsed.

"Thanks. Now come on. We've got to get those two!" I shouted as a thin stream of blood ran down my face. "You get Draz; take him hostage and get out of here. Shetvan's mine," I growled with a deep, chilling hatred. Hacea looked at me with fear. My expression softened, "It'll be all right. I'll keep us safe."

Hacea nodded. Wordlessly, we sprang.

Hacea caught Draz unaware and stunned him, and I tackled Shetvan. Hacea disappeared from the scene, leaving Shetvan and me grappling in the gory mud. The rain poured down, soaking us to the skin. Thunder boomed above us, and lightning struck near my head. The air was filled with electricity.

To my surprise, Shetvan bayed *"Mävnlick!"* and we reappeared in a pocket in one of the canyon walls. Our swords skittered to the back of the cave. We clambered up and slowly circled each other.

"So," I said coolly, "you're my brother?"

Shetvan sneered, "Unfortunately, bro."

"Why did you kill them?" I asked softly, wanting to know the truth.

"It was you," he spat bitterly. "That blizzard was meant to take only you. But I used that spell before I was ready. I never meant for it to happen. It was an accident!" Shetvan faltered a moment before putting on a mask devoid of emotion. "You are the reason they are dead! And I'll kill you for it."

Shetvan leapt at me. I raised my claws and opened my mouth to snap. I raked Shetvan's shoulder and ripped his flesh. With a muffled whine, Shetvan picked me up by the scruff of my neck and flung me against an outcropping of rock. Hard. There was a great clap of thunder. Everyone stopped and turned toward the cave as if spellbound.

I was temporarily paralyzed. I held my breath as Shetvan stalked over. He examined me closely, then retrieved my sword and laid it by my side. He thought I was dead. He walked to the entrance of the cave, watching the battle, which had resumed, and then spoke.

"At last, I have defeated my greatest enemy: my brother. I thought I would be happy, but no." At this, his voice broke, and he fell silent. Shetvan drew a deep breath. "Now, I must finish this with Hacea, who betrayed me!" Shetvan raged, using anger to block his pain.

Adrenaline, fueled by shock and fury, coursed through my blood. Creeping up like a cat, I snarled silently. My mind was clear as a mountain spring. Shadeslayer slid silently from its sheath. With his back to me, Shetvan picked up his rust-colored sword. I was breathing heavily, watching a maniacal snarl form on his tormented face. I growled like a wild beast, "Stay away from her!"

Shetvan spun around.

"Aran?"

"I am he, in flesh and blood."

"You were dead! You *should* be dead!" Shetvan shouted.

"Merely paralyzed!" I snarled, rising from a springing crouch.

I began to pace forward, and Shetvan backed up, nervously looking behind him. I slashed at Shetvan's chest with Shadeslayer, and he jumped back. His hind paw slid off the ledge, and he fell off completely as I pressed the attack. A streak of lightning flashed, setting fire to a tree. Shetvan spread his wings and looped as I soared off the cliff to face him. Without warning, I feigned a left cut but drew back and slashed hard right. Shetvan parried it with venomous fury, and we collided.

Our deadly, midair ballet drew us so close, we almost touched, but then spun us away as our blades wove a bloody, glinting web of steel. I had the upper hand, ripping his uninjured shoulder. Then, the tables turned, and Shetvan slashed my left wrist. With a deadly stroke, I clipped Shetvan's right wingtip. Howling in agony, he spiraled downward. I began to take pursuit. An unbidden finger of fear traced my spine as I heard Hacea's cry cut off.

"ARA-!"

There was a flash of lightning, and the treachery was illuminated. Draz, brandishing his bloody blade. Hacea, lying on the ground, motionless.

"No!" I screamed. I sped down to her. I killed Draz with a single blow of fury. I blocked out everything except Hacea. I knelt beside her and gently lifted her from the ground. I cried and tenderly held her in my arms, keeping her head on my shoulder.

"No! You can't die!" I sobbed hopelessly. Hacea, unconscious, didn't respond. I kissed her forehead and sheathed my sword. Taking off, I flew slowly toward Kalabar, who was fighting by the other unicorn generals. When he saw Hacea, he dropped his blade.

"No!" he whispered hoarsely. I nodded; words weren't necessary. I carefully bequeathed her to Kalabar and again drew Shadeslayer. I closed my eyes and molded every ounce of strength and emotion in my body into a single bar, stamped with one word: revenge. I cleared my mind entirely and carefully searched the battlefield. I found Shetvan laughing maniacally beside Draz's corpse.

"The battle is over, Aran. Hacea is dead, and you have lost!" he jeered wildly.

"Silence!" I commanded in a deep, passionate voice that was not quite my own. Shetvan's mouth continued to move, but no sound came out. His eyes widened with fear once more. It was then that I knew I truly had become Aran; I was speaking in the Old Tongue. "We duel here and now, brother. To the death!!!" I roared, preparing Shadeslayer for the final plunge.

Shetvan nodded, fear replaced with a fiery hatred.

We saluted each other with the tips of our swords, part of the ancient tradition encompassing the death dance we were about to commence. I jabbed Shadeslayer at Shetvan's chest, his rust-colored sword swung up to intercept it. I twirled around, brought my blade up and drove it down to pierce his heart. Shetvan barely deflected it, and we clashed.

I invented new, risky combinations as we wildly stabbed and blocked; Shetvan resorted to much trickery. I narrowly missed a kick directed at the fork of my legs by flipping backward and landing ten feet away from Shetvan.

"Bloodlust shall be the last sight you see!" taunted Shetvan.

"It ends here, but for you!" I snarled.

At the exact same moment that I leapt to rip out Shetvan's heart, Shetvan held up his palm, yelling, *"Rotc Tobesztob Scilagin ihn!"*

I drove my black blade, licked with flames, through Shetvan's chest, and he howled in agony, his green eyes bitter, wide, and wild. I whooped in triumph. Then, I collapsed as Shetvan's last magic, the red bolt of energy, smote me in the chest. My eyes rolled back in my head, and I fell unconscious.

CHAPTER TWENTY

Aftermath

I blinked and raised my paw over my eyes as the first ray of sunlight stabbed them. *Where am I? Shetvan's dead...Hacea!* I gulped, abruptly sitting up. My head blackened, and I swayed dizzily.

"Easy, milord. Easy," encouraged a familiar voice, laying a hand on my shoulder.

"Skye? What are you doing here? Were you captured?" I asked, my head still swimming as my eyes adjusted.

"No, I am a friend. I have been all along. As well as Zodrac, my friend the falcon," Skye smiled. I heard a soft chirring as a black-brown falcon with soft eyes came into my sightline. "That piece of magic you did when you killed Shetvan was very dangerous. You didn't actually speak the Old Tongue; you thought it."

That might explain why my sword was on fire, I thought.

"I'm very surprised you managed to block Shetvan's spell; it's a killer," Skye said.

I smiled.

"Yes, and it's taken all of my skill and patience to keep you all alive," Diego grumbled good-naturedly.

I looked up and down the row of cots. Among countless others, Apache was there with a gauzy snout, Demon had a bandage around his upper skull, Shadow had a casted leg, and, breathing slowly and evenly, was Hacea.

"She's all right, but her wounds will take time to heal," Zodrac assured me, ruffling her feathers on her perch.

Hacea looked so peaceful, she could have left for the Spirit Mountains.

"So, when are you going to ask her?" asked Shadow, hobbling over with a grin, Demon at his side.

"What?"

Demon rolled his eyes. "How thick are you, Wildy? When are you going to ask Hacea to marry you?" he asked in a deliberate, slow voice.

"I don't know. There's so much to be done, so little time…if she gets better, *when* she gets better, I'll ask her," I said, rolling the thought around in my head. I looked at my brothers. "Did you know Hacea has two older sisters, about your ages?"

"Oh, really?" Demon asked.

"No, but we'll look into the matter!" Shadow assured me.

They quickly withdrew and began chatting animatedly. *They totally fell for it,* I snorted softly.

"Diego, I must see Kalabar!" I insisted, realizing he must want to hear my account of the battle.

"I had a feeling you'd say that. Eat first, then we'll talk," Diego instructed, handing me a steaming bowl of amber liquid. It was a delicious beef, barley, and cattail soup. It quickly restocked my strength.

"Now?" I asked hopefully.

"You are a persistent one, aren't you, Aran?" Diego muttered in a patient way. "Put these on, and Tañgor will escort you," he instructed, eyes flicking between mine and the golden general's while tossing me a bundle of clothes.

I pulled on the soft leather jerkin and leggings, beaver-skin boots, and black cape. I belted on the elaborate scabbard and placed Shadeslayer in it. I shook my long, shaggy mane out of my eyes, following Tañgor out of the infirmary to Kalabar's fortress. The ground was muddy, and a thick, sluggish mist clogged my vision. It was early morning the next day, and no one was out or about. We proceeded to the map room.

Kalabar sat in a brown, elaborately cushioned chair at the head of the table. His left arm was in a light sling, and he had another cut above his left brow. On his face was a broad grin. "We won, Aran! We won, Shetvan's dead, and it's all thanks to you!"

I inclined my head mirthfully and sat down.

"Yes, and I see <u>you</u> have a set of matching scars!" I teased.

Kalabar snorted. "And what of you? Does that handsome scratch not count?"

My paw traced the thin scar across my cheekbone to the corner of my mouth.

"Aye, it counts. I haven't exactly seen a mirror since yesterday before the battle," I explained in wry humor.

Kalabar arched an eyebrow. "Oh?" He snapped his fingers, and Askrie produced a full-length mirror. I blinked appreciatively. The service here was excellent! The burly dapple-grey guard leaned the mirror against the wall, and I examined myself. I did a double take. Was that me?

My fur was silver, but dappled with shadow, perfect for hunting prey in the snow. My eyes were a piercing, silver blue. My claws were white, and my silver wings folded at my sides. I bared my sharp, serrated teeth. My fur perfectly showcased my muscles, and I fingered the place where the scarring process had been magically speeded. I looked so different. My coat had been grey as a cub, my face smooth and free of marks, illuminated by yellow-green eyes. Now, I looked older, mature and serious, heavy with the knowledge of the lives I had taken for my rule.

I turned back to Kalabar, and Askrie removed the mirror.

"You wish to hear my account of the battle?" I asked. Kalabar nodded, and I told him. I told him in great detail about saving Hacea, of Cherokee saving me and me repaying the favor. I described the soldier who gave me my scar, the battle in the cave, killing Draz, and the final duel with Shetvan. Kalabar listened quietly, absorbing the information. I came to the end of my tale, and then Kalabar stirred.

"I see. Aran, I need you to identify a few prisoners and tell me whether or not they can be trusted."

I nodded and followed him out a side door. Behind it was a stone dungeon. In it were Turin, Ceris, Sergeant Foxeye, Captain Drake, Lieutenant Eclipse, Red, Storm, Thunder-Eye, and Klaukos. All but the latter two kneeled.

"Well, get up! I'm not going to lop off your heads!" I informed them. As they rose, I turned to Kalabar. "Turin,

Ceris, Sergeant Foxeye, Captain Drake, Lieutenant Eclipse, Red, and Storm are trustworthy." I pointed to each of them in turn. "Hacea will have to vouch for Klaukos." I whirled and pointed at Red and Storm. "You two!"

"Yes?" they answered.

"Can you confirm my suspicion that Thunder-Eye is Draz's brother?"

To my surprise, it was Storm who first answered. "Yes, Lord Aran, he is." And when Thunder-Eye glared at her, she held her head high and responded, "I owe you no allegiance now that the desecrator has fallen. I say, long live Lord Aran! Long live the Night Warrior!"

Red nodded emphatically, and Storm smiled for the first time since I had known her. I nodded gratefully at both of them.

"Do with him as you wish," I told Kalabar as my friends were released.

"Solitary confinement," Kalabar muttered.

"He's a werewolf. Both he and Draz were the dangerous kind," I cautioned him.

Kalabar narrowed his eyes. "Human shamans?" I nodded. He stopped me and looked me in the eye. "Aran, it's time we discuss some important matters. Let us step into my private chambers."

We entered a richly decorated room, and Kalabar closed the door. He indicated a small desk with two chairs, and I sat. He did as well and leaned back in his chair and examined me.

When my patience began to fray, Kalabar finally spoke. "As you defeated Shetvan, you are now the king of Arkamish. There will be a coronation soon. You will have to choose council members. And Aran, I must know—do you intend to wed Hacea?"

I was startled. "Yes, I do, as soon as she is well. But how? My moneybag has been empty for years."

To my surprise, Kalabar burst out laughing.

"Aran, did you not expect to inherit the treasure of the castle?" he at last managed to chuckle.

I smacked my forehead. "I knew that."

Kalabar chuckled, "Ah, but you have the wit, tongue, and vocabulary of a Seer. Now, may I suggest the Day of the White Bear?"

"Four days? Why so soon?"

"I only suggest it because it is the date of Shyma and Darma's wedding. That way both ceremonies could be performed the same day," Kalabar explained.

I acquiesced to his wisdom. He didn't want the populace to be flustered, attending one royal wedding and scurrying to prepare for the next.

"Now, about my advisors," I said. "I would like to appoint Red, Storm, Shadow, Demon, Apache, Turin, and Ceris to be my council members."

Kalabar nodded thoughtfully. "Two experienced advisors, three of different race, and two commoners."

"And one or two unicorns," I hastily added, "and I will always lend my ear to you."

Clapping erupted from behind me.

"Well said, Aran. Well said."

CHAPTER TWENTY-ONE
Fallen Warrior

I whirled around. Between Dreamfighter and Diego, leaning on Dreamfighter for support and with a tired look, was Hacea, her torso bound. I rushed over and hugged her gently, kissing her cheek.

"Are you all right?" I asked, carrying her to my now-vacant chair.

Diego answered for her.

"No, she is not. But by tomorrow, she will be her, ah, frolicsome old self," Diego said.

Hacea smiled wryly at him and warmly at me.

"Hacea, I would be most grateful if you would relate your tale," Kalabar said, "up until last night and a few other matters. And there is something you should know."

Hacea sat up, curious, and I walked to the door.

"If you will excuse me, I have some business to attend to." I bowed and exited the room. I caught up to Turin and Ceris who were talking to Red and Storm, all four smiling. "May I see you two for a moment?" I said, gesturing to Turin and Ceris. The two dwarves followed me behind a tent after we said farewell to the other two. "Ceris, do you know a jeweler in Flisma?" I asked.

Ceris's eyes sparkled as she guessed my motive. "Why yes, I know her personally. She is the best in Arkamish."

I turned to Turin. "Would you accompany us to tell your friends that Aran rules once more, Arkamish is free, and Shetvan's dead?"

Turin nodded.

I spread my wings and gestured for Ceris to climb onto my back. Turin joined her.

With strong uplifts, I left the ground and soared into the sky, the rising sun warming my face. We soon arrived at Flisma, and I smoothly drifted down, carving large circles in the sky. Turin left to find some friends, and Ceris guided me to the jeweler. The sign read 'Polaris's Fine Gems'. Ceris nudged me forward, and I entered.

A very attractive female wolf was behind the counter. Polaris had red-brown fur and green eyes with a white star between them. She smiled when she saw Ceris. When she saw me, my wings still fanning the air, Polaris gasped and threw herself to the floor. I sighed before gently pulling her to her feet.

"It's all right. You don't need to be afraid," I said.

She brushed herself off and looked at the floor.

She was still nervous as she asked, "Milord, if you are king, then what of Shetvan?"

I smiled as I softly responded, "Dead by my hand."

Polaris murmured a soft prayer of thanks before turning to Ceris. "What will it be today?" Ceris leaned forward and whispered hurriedly. Polaris's eyes sparkled mischievously. "I see. Come this way."

She led us briskly to a pillar of black marble in the back of the shop. Atop the violet velvet cushion sat a ring, and I knew it was Hacea's.

Two wolves of silver with rubies for eyes formed the ring itself, while a beautiful sparkling lapis lazuli crowned the whole piece, supported by four thin legs.

"It's perfect," I said as I thanked Polaris.

"The crown will pay," Ceris interjected as she handed Polaris another ring, a wide silver band intended for me.

Polaris nodded, fetching a black velvet box for the rings. I made a mental note to be very generous with her tip.

"Polaris," I said, pocketing the box, "tell everyone. Spread the word."

She nodded, her eyes glistening with tears of joy.

The streets were already filling with people as one of Turin's friends shouted the news. Turin jumped onto my back, pulling Ceris with him. "Long live Lord Aran! Long live Lord Aran!"

The cheers of the people reached our ears as we sped toward the camp.

"They will never forget today. It shall be a national holiday!" Turin assured me as I set down on the ground.

"If anyone comes looking for me, tell them I am busy, unless it's urgent."

The dwarves nodded and departed. I pocketed the ring and slunk back to my tent. I tied the latch so no one would burst inside and retrieved the Orb, which I had hidden under the basin the previous night.

I removed the charcoal-colored cloak and set the Orb on the basin. Feeling a bit foolish, I stated clearly, "I wish to speak with Shamar and Klemore Freerunner!"

The Orb swirled and then disappeared. A smoky mirror took its place. "Mom! Dad!" I whispered. They stepped out of the mirror, and I rushed forward to embrace them. Then, I stepped back and looked them each in the eye. "Tell me the whole truth. How is Shetvan my brother, Hacea my half-sister, and why didn't you tell me?"

My father looked at my mother, and she nodded. My father took a deep breath, and the story unfolded. "I fathered you and Shetvan with my old girlfriend Crescent." My mother gave him a disapproving look, and he laughed nervously. Then he turned and gave me a disapproving look. "Sound familiar, Wildy?" And it was my turn to laugh nervously. "Your mother and I had Shadow, Demon, and Hacea. Crescent wanted me to fully adopt you and Shetvan because she had five other pups to look after, and we had only three. Then, when you were about four weeks old, Shetvan and Hacea were spirited away by a hunting party from Maketur. Shetvan was raised in Guilyed, separate from Hacea. Hacea was raised with two other wolves whom she knows as her sisters. We didn't tell you because, well…we didn't think you were ready."

"Ah." They had discovered what Star and I had been doing on our last visit.

Taking a deep breath, I looked at my parents. "Now you have answered my questions, I may answer one of yours. It's my intention, if… ."

I stopped short and spun around because Hacea rushed in, snapping the latch, with her armor on, Sunchaser drawn. "Aran! Come quickly!" She paused. "Are those our parents?"

I nodded, and, turning a tad more toward my parents, I knelt on one knee. "If you, Shamar and Klemore, agree to it, then it is my intention to wed Hacea." Here, the other three gasped as I pulled out the ring. "Hacea, will you say yes?"

Hacea's eyes were filled with tears of happiness. "Yes, Wilder. Yes."

I stood and kissed her, and for the first time, she really kissed me back. We stood for a moment, then Hacea's eyes snapped open.

"Aran, we must go! A group of rogue dragons and some others have cornered Gruffin! We have to help!" she said.

My eyes burned. "Mom, Dad, I have to go! We'll see each other again!" I promised, spreading my wings and readying Shadeslayer.

They nodded, and Hacea and I took off. Shyma, Dreamfighter, and Cherokee followed us.

The dragons had pinned Gruffin to the cliff and were forcing him almost off the edge when we arrived. A Minotaur, some bedraggled looking manticores, and a one-armed ogre turned to fight us off. Hacea tackled the manticores, I got the other two, and our companions began hacking at the dragons.

When at last the three dragons lay dying, Gruffin stood to leave. Then, before I could stop it, the last dragon used the remnants of its strength to push Gruffin off the edge before it perished. I flew as quickly as I could to where Gruffin's prone form lay heaving. He coughed up blood, and his breathing became ragged.

"Gruffin? Can you hear me?" I whispered.

He grimaced bitterly, "Yes, I can. But not for long." Gruffin coughed up more blood.

"It's okay, big guy. You're gonna make it. Just hold on!" I soothed.

Gruffin laughed softly. "This is what I get for playing the hero, you idiot. I'm dying."

I shook my head, readying the magic.

Gruffin reached out and grabbed my arm with a single claw and a miniscule smile. "No."

The others arrived by a path along the cliffside. I began sobbing.

"Farewell, Aran. Thank you," Gruffin gasped, "that I may die a free dragon."

He took his last breath and was still. I buried my head in his shoulder. Hacea knelt by my side, holding me in her arms. We all wept. At last I stood, sheathed my blade, and faced my companions.

"How can fate be so cruel as to tear from us a brave warrior at the height of our triumph? But a brave warrior he was, so fear not to show your tears! Rather, let them flow freely! All will mourn Gruffin the Free!" I said, and turned back to the corpse of the great blue dragon and stroked his cheek. "You will be avenged, brother."

Hacea, Dreamfighter, Shyma, and I wove a litter of tree branches with magic and carried Gruffin back to the ruins where he had dwelt. There we buried him. We quickly returned to camp. Kalabar met us at the entrance. Scanning our ranks, he bowed his head.

"Come, I have news," I said.

Kalabar followed me to a tree. Checking to see that we were alone, I leaned forward and whispered, "Kalabar, I searched the mind of one of those dragons. They were under orders from Thunder-Eye!"

Kalabar's eyes closed. When they opened, his blue eyes a storm in an icy sea, I knew. This was how Honeysuckle had died. Cornered, rescued, and struck down by a dying foe. And Kalabar couldn't summon the power to save her as she died in his arms. He, too, had promised to avenge her death.

"He's yours, Kalabar. I've had my own revenge. A duel to the death," I told him.

Kalabar nodded with a heavy heart. He left to gather his armor and sword, and I stayed to tell the others.

CHAPTER TWENTY-TWO

Hacea, Will You Say...?

"Come on, let's go," I said, trotting to the clearing where the duel was to be held. Already, the area had been marked with stakes and rope. Peltshifter was waiting in one corner with borrowed armor and his sword.

Kalabar entered from the other corner.

"Aran, how did you know? About Honeysuckle?" Hacea asked me after I had told her about the conversation with Kalabar.

I looked into her copper eyes and tried to explain. "I saw the loss in his eyes...I just knew."

Hacea understood. Then, we turned to the square. The duel had begun.

The werewolf began a dizzying ballet of lunging and parrying. It was a blur as the two crossed blades, sparring for several minutes. At last the swordfight slowed as both expressed a need to catch their breath. Thunder-Eye looked like he was preparing to sidestep and thrust when Kalabar, mustering every iota of speed and skill he possessed, thrust his sword into the chest of Thunder-Eye, who staggered for a moment before his eyes rolled back in his head, and he crumpled into the dust. Kalabar stabbed his foe once more in the heart, and raised his sword in victory. The crowd cheered with a savage energy; they knew Honeysuckle had been avenged.

I found my arm back around Hacea's shoulder, and I whispered in her ear, "We'll have to do that all over again in front of them, you know."

She looked at me and nodded.

Thunder-Eye's corpse was removed to be burned, and all who had commanded and fought in the last battle met in the map room.

In the map room, I whispered to Askrie, and he left the room. "It is with great sorrow that I tell you of the death of Gruffin, our friend and fellow commander. From this day forward, he shall be known as Gruffin the Free," I announced.

Startled, I looked to Apache as he keened his sorrow to the skies, and Cherokee joined him. When at last they were silent, tears were in their eyes.

"He was my blood brother," Apache explained.

"And mine as well," Cherokee echoed.

I patted Apache on the shoulder. "It'll be all right, Apache. I've lost friends, too, and I'm still here."

Askrie stepped back into the room, so I turned to Hacea and knelt. "Hacea, will you marry me?" I asked.

Hacea lifted me up and smiled, "Yes, Aran. Yes!"

We kissed once more, and everyone clapped and wolf-whistled. Askrie came forward as we stepped apart, and I turned to Kalabar.

"In gratitude for all that you have done for me, for Arkamish, and for her people, I would like to present to you an artifact. It will allow you to communicate with your lost one." Here I paused and uncovered it. "The Orb of the Eagle's Eye." I pressed it into Kalabar's hands, his eyes shining.

"Thank you, Aran. You have no idea what it means to me and my family."

I looked him straight in the eyes, and Kalabar knew that I knew. He smiled, and the wedding preparations were begun.

Shyma and I waited at the altar as Darma and Hacea stood by the door, waiting for the music to start. Shyma wore a silver uniform with a silver cape and a gold circlet on his brow. He wore white epaulets, his sword in a creamy scabbard and belt. His black mane, tail, and coat were groomed to perfection, and his black horn hummed with energy.

I wore a black shirt and pants, silver vest and a half-cape over my shoulder. A silver crown, studded with lapis lazulis, was over my ears, and Shadeslayer hung in a charcoal-leather scabbard and belt. My silver coat glistened. I fingered the hilt of my blade as the music began, and our brides stepped down the aisle, side by side.

Darma's misty blue gown was trimmed with emerald embroideries. Her silver tiara had a single, radiant star sapphire in the center. Her flowing mane had been braided with misty blue ribbons, and she took her place across from Shyma.

Hacea wore a dress the color of honey with light pink satin sleeves. A ruby necklace hung on her chest. She wore a golden tiara studded with three garnets, and her eyes were more mesmerizing than when we had first met.

We exchanged rings. Hacea and Darma said their vows first, then Shyma and I.

At last, the priest proclaimed, "You may kiss the brides."

Hacea leaned forward, and I embraced and kissed her.

Cheers and wolf-whistles filled the chapel when the four of us lifted our hands and shouted, "Let the feast begin!"

That day of the White Bear will not soon be forgotten.

Guilyed was rechristened Sörryllö. Hacea and I lived there, and Kalabar, Shyma, and Darma took up residence at Wildspirit Castle. The ruins Gruffin had called home were refurbished, and Apache, Cherokee, and other dragons reside there. A proper graveyard was constructed around Gruffin the Free. Kalabar frequently visited Honeysuckle with the Orb of the Eagle's Eye, and I was introduced to her. But that is a story for another time.

In time, Shyma and Darma had twins: Adönia, a blue roan like her grandfather, Kalabar, and Bruán, a black Appaloosa like his father. Believe it or not, both were Unici.

Shadow married Lilia, one of Hacea's sisters, and Demon is still chasing after Polaris.

I've heard that Red and Storm are getting quite serious.

And I…I finally finished *Fire Storm*. It depicted the tale of another Aran and Shetvan saga. Shetvan had burned all the copies because he feared it foretold <u>his</u> destruction. I quickly republished the book, and soon it became a popular read all over the kingdom.

Hacea, in time, had four pups. Angel was a beautiful cream color with white markings, gold eyes, and white paws. She was kind, loving, and a tomboy to the end.

Kornak was grey and black with blue eyes and big paws suited for crossing marshy land. He was quiet, very smart, and a genius with a mace.

General was a muscular, black-furred wolf with green eyes and a white bar across his shoulders. He was very athletic, cocky, and a great hunter and warrior.

Then there was Arrel. Arrel was a beautiful silver and red wolf. Her paws, legs, throat, belly, and face were silver-white. Her back, tail, neck, ears, and forehead were red. Her eyes were a cool silver. She was gorgeous, as beautiful as her mother. She was kind, fiery, instinctive, and as much a tomboy as Angel.

Soon after that, I took my charger, Altäi, and visited Star. Sure enough, I returned with two of our eight pups, both boys, born on the same day as Hacea's litter.

Donier was a light brown with dark brown markings and mask. He was cold, lofty, and calculating, and constantly bore watching.

Mírak was the true image of a prince. Strong yet streamlined, he had reddish white fur, a chocolate muzzle, and white paws and chest. He was wise and an excellent woodsman, swordsman, archer, and warrior, the spitting image of his father.

Of course, for their birthdays, I bought each a horse. Angel's mare was named Orion, who was blacker than the night with a gold mane, tail, and feathering.

Mírak's stallion, Fledge, was a red dun with black mane, tail, muzzle, stockings, and feathering with wall eyes.

Arrel's mare, Jinx, was a sandy brown with bronze mane, tail, and feathering.

General's stallion, Irish, was a handsome orange chestnut with flaxen mane, tail, and feathering and a blaze that covered his muzzle.

Kornak's mare, Dancer, was pure white with blue eyes and a black muzzle.

Donier's stallion was a black, heavy boned creature with thick black mane, tail, and feathering. He was almost as cold as his master, who called him Destrier.

My Altäi was a blackish brownish appaloosa with grey eyes. He held his head high, like a king's horse should. He was regal and swift and feared nothing.

Hacea's mare, Falcon, was a buckskin with a sandy mane, tail, and feathering. She was very swift and an excellent jumper and hunter.

Once in a while, we held competitions. There was a hunt in the morning, noonmeal at midday by the stream, and a race back to Sörryllö. We all spent at least two times in the winner's circle, even Kornak. Ah, the battles between Mírak and Donier, or rather Fledge and Destrier, were fierce, and Donier spent *only* twice in the winner's circle. And one of their quarrels…but my tale has come to a close.

Farewell, my friends. Safe travels, and may the Spirits watch over you.

CPSIA information can be obtained at www.ICGtesting.com
Printed in the USA
LVOW08s1909071013

355848LV00001B/3/P